D1639305

ACKNOWLEDGMENTS

It was a great experience to work with Oliver Stone on the film and book WALL STREET; his devotion to film, professionalism and friendship are much appreciated. I am grateful to Oliver, producers Alex Ho and Ed Pressman and Twentieth Century Fox for encouraging me to step out of my normal milieu and write fiction.

Many friends provided advice and good judgment. I wish to thank Joseph Heller, Kurt Vonnegut, Mort Janklow, Jerry Wexler and Professor Sidney Offit for devoting considerable time and skills to my effort.

Thanks to my parents for getting me to Wall Street in the first place, and to Lehman Brothers and Salomon Brothers for providing me with such a fulfilling career on the Street.

My wife Evelyn and my four daughters suffered missed vacations and broken promises during the writing process. Their good humor and support were vital to this project. Peggy Smith, my devoted assistant, was a stalwart in getting the book through drafts and redrafts.

Berkley books, particularly Publisher Roger Cooper and Executive Editor Jayne Pliner, were miracle workers in overcoming logistical problems and getting this book published on short notice; their success was generally the result of optimism, hard work and a solid organization behind them.

MICHAEL DOUGLAS CHARLIE SHEEN DARYL HANNAH

Every dream has a price.

AN OLIVER STONE FILM

WALL STREET

TWENTIETH CENTURY FOX PRESENTS

· AN EDWARD R. PRESSMAN PRODUCTION ·

AN OLIVER STONE FILM

MICHAEL DOUGLAS · CHARLIE SHEEN

DARYL HANNAH · MARTIN SHEEN

WALL STREET

HAL HOLBROOK AND TERENCE STAMP

ORIGINAL MUSIC BY STEWART COPELAND   DIRECTOR OF PHOTOGRAPHY ROBERT RICHARDSON

CO-PRODUCER A. KITMAN HO   WRITTEN BY STANLEY WEISER & OLIVER STONE

PRODUCED BY EDWARD R. PRESSMAN   DIRECTED BY OLIVER STONE

For Michael Bennett and Jeff Byers—
Creativity and Friendship Untimely Taken

WALL STREET

CHAPTER I

Being a crook was the most exciting time in Bud Fox's Wall Street career. His descent into crime started June 15, 1985, on the steps of a New York City subway station.

$ $ $

As on every other weekday, Fox stopped at the subway entrance to buy *The Wall Street Journal*. Both he and the Pakistani merchant to whom he handed fifty cents moved so swiftly and mechanically through their daily ritual that neither had uttered a single word to the other in three years. The young man bought a cinnamon donut and a container of regular coffee from a street vendor at the head of the staircase and gulped it down as he plunged into the

1

cavernous subway station. Even the dreaded rush-hour subway ride from Seventy-second Street and Broadway to Wall Street did not diminish Buddy's energy and enthusiasm; "Great combat training for 'the Street,'" he mused confidently.

Buddy was wearing his dark gray Paul Stuart suit with the faint red pinstripe, white shirt, red silk rep tie, and black wingtip shoes. He puzzled over why such expensive uniforms were mandatory dress for his job, when the torrid pace and pressure of work required that he remove the jacket, roll up his sleeves, and loosen the tie. "I'm not going to be the one to challenge the conventions. Go along . . . to get along," he shrugged.

Fox pushed his way through the turnstile and was compressed in the center of a huge crowd, packed around seemingly invisible markers on the subway platform. Years of anxious waiting had taught the straphangers where the subway doors would open.

The Seventh Avenue express roared into the station. Grafitti screamed from the side of every car, lest anyone forget that things were out of control. The passengers' collective unconscious incorporated fear of The Pusher, a demon who randomly expressed his rage by bumping a human sacrifice under the iron monster. The crowd retreated in unison from the platform edge. Buddy was carried effortlessly along, still reading *The Wall Street Journal*, while each person maintained his relative position.

As subway doors flew open, rush-hour passengers

were hurled onto the platform by the force of the human bellows behind them. The mob on the platform asserted its will to occupy the same space that was being evacuated before the escapees could discharge themselves through the narrow doors. Briefcase blows to the kneecaps, glancing shots at the groin, and crunching eyeglasses announced the slamming together of the offensive and defensive lines. There were no referees. Only the repeated opening and closing of the subway's steel doors helped bring an end to the match.

Fox hugged the tiny turf he now occupied in the car, cursing the stragglers who delayed him by wedging their arms and legs between the closing steel doors. Thirty seconds later, as if a silent whistle were heard, the losers fell back and the sardine-packed subway screeched out of the station.

As the mass undulated in place, Buddy positioned an attaché case between his legs, freed his hands from his sides, and started reading the *Journal* subway-style. He noticed that he was one of the few passengers reading a financial newspaper. "One fuckup and I'll be back in Queens with the rest of them," he shuddered.

The newspaper was compactly folded into sixteenths. Only the story he read lay exposed at an angle above the sea of heads around him. Bud was pleased at having mastered this trademark of veteran New Yorkers—making it work under any circumstances.

3

As Buddy read the "What's News" wrap-up column on the front of *The Wall Street Journal*, the words "Jackson & Steinhem . . . sell" jumped off the printed page.

> Jackson & Steinhem, the prestigious investment banking partnership, agreed to sell 100% of its interests to Temperance Insurance for $1.2 billion. The investment bank cited a need for capital in increasingly volatile markets and its desire to implement a global strategy. Temperance plans to market its life insurance through an expanded Jackson & Steinhem sales force. Ten of thirty Jackson & Steinhem partners resigned. Eighty-four-year-old Hiram Jackson warned greed will destroy the temple.

Buddy's heart stopped. He steadied himself by unconsciously clutching the shoulder of an elderly lady standing next to him. Thoughts raced through his confused brain. *This can't be true . . . the* Journal *is gospel . . . no discussion, no appeal . . . It's over! There goes the partnership . . . I'm doomed to be an employee forever . . . just like Dad.*

Buddy recalled with bitter irony his father's advice on accepting Jackson & Steinhem's offer in the face of higher competitive bids: "Forget money . . . go to an old-line firm that everybody's heard of. You'll become a partner, and everyone will automatically respect you."

His thoughts were shoved aside as the subway came to a grinding halt. A twenty-minute ride had taken its usual forty-five minutes. Buddy was exhausted and dripping with sweat at 8:30 A.M. His shirt clung to his back, and his suit was wrinkled like aged skin. He climbed the steep iron stairs and emerged onto Wall Street.

Buddy's expression made him look an older man; his gait was slower, his stride less sure. For the first time in three years he glanced back at the emptying station and shook his head in disgust.

"For Christ's sake, it shouldn't be this hard. Not after all I put in. For what? To sweat my balls off in a hot subway, so I can get my brains beat out at Jackson & Steinhem."

Buddy marched, bleary-eyed across William Street with a grim-faced army of pedestrians. Absorbed in rereading the story, he picked his way between bumper-to-bumper yellow cabs and cars, oblivious to the angry horns and cries of "Wake up, asshole!" Without noticing, he passed the bag lady with twelve cats, crossing herself as she looked toward Trinity Church in thanks for her bountiful collections last night.

The narrow streets of the financial district twisted and turned to arrive at the corner of Wall and Broad streets. Buddy paused to cross the street. Within his sight was America's answer to the Parthenon, pyramids, and Jerusalem, all at one intersection—the Treasury Building, Morgan Guaranty Trust Company, and the New York Stock Exchange. He had always admired the permanence and power of these institutions. At the apex of Wall Street soared the spires of

Trinity Church, giving legitimacy to God's hand in man's work.

Buddy detected the faint scent of death in the midst of these apparently immortal institutions. Erased from surrounding façades were the names of fallen angels, the weak or greedy that had been forced to close or merge. There were no memorials to Lehman Brothers, Hayden Stone, DuPont Glore Forgan, Kuhn Loeb, Walston & Co., Loeb Rhoades, Shields, Goodbody & Co., White Weld, Halsey Stuart, or McDonald & Co. Now Jackson & Steinhem joined the invisible roll of honor.

$ \quad $ $ \quad $ $

Jackson & Steinhem's twelve-story, Civil War vintage-carved limestone headquarters dominated a small alleyway just off Broad Street. Its architectural subtlety and substance lived in an uneasy truce with the power of the forty-story glass skyscraper overlooking it.

It was well documented by the press that more than half of Jackson & Steinhem's thirty partners made over $1 million per year, with the rest in the high six figures. However, each partner was only allowed to withdraw $200,000 in annual salary, with the remainder being plowed back into the firm's capital. At $600 million in capital, Jackson & Steinhem was a large private investment bank, although small compared to public competitors such as Merrill Lynch and Salomon Brothers.

Buddy valued the discreet, personalized style of the hundred-and-ten-year-old banking house. He could learn from others, participate in the community, and shape himself into a gentleman of culture and worldly dimension. From the firm had come two cabinet officers, countless presidential advisers, and board members for the world's leading corporations and nonprofit institutions. Everyone who counted knew that Jackson & Steinhem selected its partners carefully, based on character as well as merit. Investiture guaranteed respectability.

Buddy entered the stone lobby, threw away the newspaper, and jammed his body into a crowded elevator. Blank faces stared ahead, each lost in private thoughts. If eyes accidentally met, they quickly flicked away. The elevator finally came to a slow stop.

Buddy passed a cheerful-looking, young black secretary. "How you doing, Buddy?"

"Not so great . . . did you read the newspapers today?"

Carol's hidden contempt for the system, as a black person who was always left out of the action anyway, bubbled just beneath the surface.

"Don't worry about all these goings-on. They don't affect folks like us one bit. Few partners quit, bunch stay . . . all of them get richer. We stay the same, except I hear insurance companies have great employee benefit plans."

He was taken aback by Carol's sarcasm.

Buddy entered the trading floor not knowing what to expect. Least of all did he expect to find the business-as-usual atmosphere that greeted him.

A low din enveloped the trading room, like morning fog rolling off a lake to cover the countryside; except on a trading floor there was no sun to burn it off—it never lifted. Tapes whizzed around the perimeters; Dow Jones and Reuters newsprinters chattered, and teletype machines sputtered; loudspeakers roared; and human voices alternately informed, begged, demanded, and excused. As Buddy emerged onto the floor, the sales manager, Hy Lynch, was on the horn booming the suggested house menu.

"Look sharp today, boys. The Nikkei Index closed up ninety points last night. We expect heavy Japanese buying on the opening. The firm has 200,000 Steel for sale; one million Big Blue; 350,000 Pork and Beans. We're looking for 150,000 ARCO and 100,000 Mickey Mouse. Get on the horn with your institutions and report on their appetites for Commonwealth. This utility is our top priority today—firm's lead underwriting manager, and we've got to move it out. Check your manifold on computer page A-6 for the story. Harry indicates that interest rates have stopped backing up here; go out on the yield curve. We're looking to repo $100 million Fannie Maes; report any interest. Okay, let's get to work."

The uninterrupted flow of space in the block-square trading room gave the impression of an enclosed Roman forum, but the population density was more reminiscent of a Macao houseboat colony. A thousand white plastic cubicles stretched wall to wall, bolted together without any barrier above eye level. It was hard to conceive that in this horde were the most educated, talented, and well-paid professionals in America.

Information flow was the lifeblood of Jackson & Steinhem. Brokers and traders were only semiautonomous links in a huge data network. Six computer terminals stacked in each cubicle displayed constantly updated information on equities, currencies, metals, bonds, mortgages, and CDs. Each workstation had a built-in, ninety-line, turret telephone system, with a black mounted receiver on an extruded hook. Telephone lights, arrested on hold, blinked continuously The relentless blinking, amalgamated with flashing multicolored pie charts, bar graphs, and linear analyses on the omnipresent computer screens, created a sense of risk and tension usually reserved for air control towers.

"Wake up! Pick up those lights. The goddamn phones are ringing off the hook."

"Jack, pick up on two. Pru wants color on the Tokyo market close. Joe, where is the July platinum contract trading?"

"Pick up six. Alliance is getting out of oils."

"Dreyfus wants an open line at 12:45 when we start to fix the bids for the Treasury auction."

Brokers bought and sold stock for customers. Traders, like croupiers in a casino, made markets for the house. The shouting never stopped: "Research just pulled the thrifts from our recommended list . . . Sell . . . Dump it all! . . . 50,000 at an eighth, an eighth! . . ."

Traders and brokers, all wrapped in a collective high . . . until burn-out. Few gray hairs graced the floor. Beyond the daily pressure, a cloud hung over every person in the big room. Make a big financial score by thirty-five or forty years old . . . or else.

Buddy's near lifeless form slid into his swivel chair, barely avoiding being run down by brokers, sales assistants, order clerks, runners, and partners, dodging each other in the crowded aisles. He helplessly sank into the engulfing tide, ritualistically reaching for the blinking lights, lifting the receiver, and succumbing to the selling habit.

"Jack got 30,000 with a three-eighths top, forget the hundred . . . traders say I can go long at twenty-three . . . you own it . . . Monsanto, hang on, I'll check. Up a quarter. How many you want? . . . Hold! Joan, 40,000 Monsantos for Teachers' Retirement. Not held. Work it on the Exchange floor."

Buddy suddenly turned his attention to Marvin Wycoff. The prematurely balding, bespectacled thirty-two-year-old broker had shared a cubicle with Buddy for the past three years. Abrupt, swift movements reflected Marvin's manic personality as he paced at the end of a short telephone cord. Indeed, as one glazed across the trading floor, hundreds of young men and women seemed suspended from telephone cords, weathervanes trapped in a spastic wind-borne dance.

"They fucked us, Marv. Volatility, globalization . . . Bullshit! Mr. Steinhem called it right! Greed!"

"No offense, Buddy, but don't take it so personally. Straight business."

Fox was taken aback by Marvin's indifference.

"Took four generations to build Jackson & Steinhem's reputation and relationships. This generation of partners stole the premium right out from under the retired partners and future generations. Pocketed a cool $1.2 billion."

Wycoff was unmoved by Buddy's sociological perspective.

"Look, I think we can make some good money with Temperance. They'll take the firm into the rich man's business. We'll be selling stocks and insurance to wealthy individuals, at decent commissions for a change."

Wycoff thought for a moment. "Times have changed since fixed commissions ended. Can't make any money dealing with institutions under negotiated commissions of three cents and four cents a share. We're dying! I hear the giant institutions will soon start trading with each other directly by computer linkup, cutting out the middleman altogether. Our deal may be sad, but it's smart."

"Marv, is money all you can think about? We lost everything. We're part of a conglomerate. Clerks in a financial supermarket. I've been sitting next to you

for three fuckin' years... watching you carry on
... now you have something to complain about and
you're passive. I don't understand.

"Look over your shoulder, how down Billy Glass
is. He was promised a partnership this September for
building the junk bond department. He was bored
with the business and stayed around only for the
partnership—eleven years. Three months away
from financial independence, power, and prestige...
overnight, salaried insurance company clerk. Does
that make sense, Marv?"

Wycoff retreated into an annoyed but cool, practical tone of voice. "I never bought the bullshit that
you did, that I had something to say, that I would be
one of the anointed—a partner! Look, Buddy boy, I
can't afford to be a philosopher. Wife, two kids in
private school, mortgage, and alimony. Yeah, money
is kind of important to me. It's called making a living."

Dan Hickey rose from the opposite side of the
four-man cubicle, becoming visibly more agitated.
He was a large man in a black double-breasted suit,
with a red carnation pinned on his wide lapel. While
almost everyone else worked in shirtsleeves, Dan and
the "old pro," Lou Manheim, kept their jackets on
and ties up tight against starched white shirts. Hickey
was one of the few survivors from the "Irish Mafia"
that dominated the firm in the late 1940s. Dan's
flushed face betrayed his weakness.

"Get out while you're young, kid. I came here one day, I sat down, and look at me now," he said in an unusually sober tone.

"Oh, knock it off, Danny," said Chuck Cushing, a thin branch of an old family tree. "Names change, owners come and go, but things stay essentially the same. So long as the firm supports my whims—fly fishing, golf, shooting, and eighteen-year-old models —I'm happy. You guys are miserable because you think too much."

"Don't worry, Dan, I'll get over it. Once I get back into the sales pace, I'll be happy," Bud said unconvincingly.

Hickey was upset. "On Wall Street, selling stocks is all that counts. Every day is a blank sheet of paper. You'll always be too anxious about tomorrow to be able to enjoy today's success. You're a sales machine —you produce until you can't anymore, then they junk you."

Hickey didn't even realize that he was now screaming.

"Without a dream, you'll invent one. Then, watch out! You're a believer and that's dangerous. Get out!"

Buddy quietly left his seat to approach Lou Manheim, senior partner in charge of the trading floor for almost three decades. Lou liked Buddy because he was self-made; formal education had not ruined the kid's notions of institutional loyalty. Bud Fox was considered old-style Jackson & Steinhem material.

The "old pro" long ago refused a private office. He decided to run a field headquarters among the troops, from a small desk at the front of the sprawling trading room. The white-haired, slender sixty-year-old spent his day "walking and talking," the essence of a business where information was like oxygen.

Manheim was a fundamental investor, weaned on the textbook financial analysis techniques taught in Graham and Dodd. He scoffed at inside information, story stocks, and fashions. Some of the younger traders nicknamed Lou "iron balls," a grudging accolade to his ability to ride out cycles and trends—"coining money through patience," he used to say. Lou Manheim felt uncomfortable with the hot new breed of traders. For the first time in forty years with Jackson & Steinhem, Lou had talked of retirement. His mood was sullen.

"Mr. Manheim, how did *this* happen?"

"Bigness and high salaries, Buddy, those are the cancers. The firm grew because everyone else did. . . . Institutional suicide. Before anyone knew it, each day we opened the door, the fixed nut was $20 million. That's a lot of transactions . . . *every day!* The answer—bigger trading risks to cover the overhead, and London and Tokyo offices to find new markets . . . more people, more risk, more capital . . . more overhead."

14

Manheim looked worn as he continued.

"The Temperance offer came along, and a tidal wave of fear and greed seized the partnership, with everyone's total wealth tied up here. In a peculiar way, I'm glad to be an old man."

CHAPTER II

One hundred and ten years of Jackson & Steinhem tradition withered before the onslaught of depersonalization and pressures to cover mushrooming overhead. Temperance Insurance doubled the firm's size. The two-story trading room was decked to accommodate the growth, creating the claustrophobic feeling of a Middle Eastern bazaar.

Time sheets, hierarchical structures, budget projections, circulars on dress and demeanor, employee fraternization rules, expense reports, transportation forms, restraining manuals, and sales quotas became the fare of a bureaucracy exploding in size and power. Television cameras were placed in newly suspended ceilings. Microphones were installed in every salesperson's receiver, so that all calls could be recorded, ostensibly to reduce litigation by customers. Managers could monitor any conversation undetected. The assault on the rich man's business was systematized. Computerized cold-call lists and zip code telephone books were handed to each account executive, divided by alphabet. Bud was targeted on Gs, Ga–Ge.

Bud was nervous and fearful. "I'll never survive. I gotta make it; no choice. Adjust! Transactions, not relationships, count. Forget institutional culture — action. Keep on dialing for dollars!" he kept telling himself.

Buddy removed his diplomas and ski trophy from the back of his cubicle and placed them in a bottom drawer.

"Hey, what are you doing?" Marvin exclaimed with genuine surprise.

"Nobody ever asks you about the schools you attended or the sports you excelled at after your first job interviews. All that counts on Wall Street is how many tickets you write."

The telephone light interrupted the conversation. "Buddy, pick up on seventy-two; it's Mr. Roach."

"Sonofabitch, says he didn't order the hundred CQS options."

Buddy picked up on Harold Roach, one of the wealthy prospects assigned to him by the firm.

"Hey, Harold. You must have forgotten. Remember, you said your printer gave you a hot tip to buy CQS? I hardly even heard of the stock. Sure, it's gone down a little bit. I didn't tell you to buy it, so why should I tell you to sell it?"

Harold replied calmly. "I don't care. Give it back . . . let Jackson & Steinhem eat the loss."

Buddy's head pulsed with frustration. "No, I can't give it back! Give it back to who? You own it! No, he's out right now."

Hy Lynch, the middle-aged sales manager, appeared like an apparition looking over his shoulder. "Give me that phone," he grimaced, grabbing the receiver from Bud. "I'm in charge here. What seems to be the problem, Mr. Roach?"

Bud whispered tensely to Lynch as the sales manager listened to Roach, nodding. "He's lying, Mr. Lynch, he's lying."

"Okay, sir. I'll discuss it with the account executive, and I'll get back to you. You're very welcome."

He released the call button and turned on Buddy. "I'm closing out this account. If he doesn't pay for it tomorrow, you pay for it."

"Mr. Lynch, I swear to you, he's lying."

"Fox, we gave you one of those 'rich man' accounts, and you tell me he DK'd you for a lousy quarter point?"

"I don't think you're being fair, sir. You assigned me this guy, and you know he's got a history . . ."

Lynch dropped his head almost unnoticeably, his left eye twitching slightly. "Fox, this ain't the old days when the firm ate such losses. Are we going to sue him? Lawyers' fees cost more than the claim.

Somebody has to pay for the error, and it's not going to be me. You pay . . . understand!"

Lynch clutched the bull's head at the top of his recently acquired wooden cane, shaking his head slowly as he painfully walked off. The blue-suited figure bowed reluctantly to this prop, as gout swelled through his throbbing foot.

"Fox, you cause more problems around here than you make sales. Wake up, or. . ."

Buddy stood stunned, his mouth parched, except for an acidic taste that rose from his esophagus. It wasn't clear whether the monetary damage or the humiliation of being first cheated then betrayed was more galling.

"I gotta get out of here, Marv . . . be on the other end of that phone. I have to do something where individual effort counts, not this perverse bureaucratic bullshit."

"Go slow, Buddy. It's no bed of roses out there either."

CHAPTER III

Three years ago, Bud Fox had taken the longest trip in the United States, across the Fifty-ninth Street Bridge between Queens and Manhattan.

Buddy had seldom left Queens before college. His image of the Big Apple was a relic of schooldays, subconsciously shaped by class trips. The Museum of Natural History made evolution seem inevitably progressive. The Hayden Planetarium dazzled the little black and white faces of schoolchildren with the message that you can fly in space. The Metropolitan Museum showed that rich people historically enjoyed elegant furniture, jewelry, and paintings, while the Museum of Modern Art proved such elegance was available today.

Harvard Business School had not eradicated

Buddy's romantic spirit. He returned to New York high on *The Fountainhead*. Buddy walked in the footsteps of Howard Roark, Ayn Rand's desperately ambitious architect-hero, from Hell's Kitchen to the corner of Central Park.

"I'll take it all," he echoed Roark. "It's mine."

The lights twinkled invitingly to him from their owners' $3 million Fifth Avenue apartment windows; the stretch limos lined up in front of canopied doors soon recognized their natural master; and the fashionable international set that floated carelessly in and out of the Sherry Netherland waited patiently for Mr. Fox to arrive.

Buddy had grounds for optimism. His ambition had been well honed and rewarded during his twenty-six years. He was the son of an airline mechanic, valedictorian, and winner of scholarships to Dartmouth and Harvard Business School. Fox saw his first pair of skis at seventeen, made ski patrol at nineteen, and won the Sugarbush downhill races before college graduation.

Earnings of $50,000 per year enabled Buddy to afford a one-bedroom walk-up on Seventy-fifth Street, between Columbus and Amsterdam avenues. The comfortable one-family brownstone had been subdivided into nine apartments, including the studio in the basement. The pigeon droppings that speckled the deteriorating sandstone face gave the brownstone a sad and friendless look. Buddy was nevertheless grateful to get his 972 square feet of living space in overcrowded Manhattan for only $1100 per month. He told his mother that this was temporary, until he could get the cash to move across Central Park to the chic Upper East Side.

Now that Buddy lived in the correct zip code, 10024 New York, New York, he had neither the time nor the energy, let alone the money, for theaters, restaurants, and all-night clubs. With homework— charts, economic statistics, computer runs, technical analyses, and research reports—he had become a quantitative monk. Like so many holy men, Buddy felt he was sacrificing for the next life—as a respected and affluent partner of Jackson & Steinhem. His dream of becoming an owner was shattered by the sale of Jackson & Steinhem; like his father, Bud would work for a large corporation.

Although Buddy was lonely and poor in Manhattan, his mood was careless when he walked down the streets of Queens. While the streets of Manhattan demanded an identity card, the pavement in Sunnyside rose to meet his footsteps, as if in familiar greeting from the old neighborhood.

$ $ $

He parked his 1983 Honda Civic in front of his parents' red-brick two-family home. The grassy quarter acre on which it sat was parted by a narrow walk, which ended in two brick steps against a white wooden front door. Buddy rang the bell. Nobody answered. His mother must be off doing errands, God knew where. But he knew just where to find his father.

Down the street Buddy passed Birnbaum's Deli. Mr. Birnbaum bellowed, "Good afternoon, Buddy," from the doorway of the shop, above the noise of a portable television propped on a card table. "How's Dad?"

"Pretty good. I'm going over to see him at McGregor's Bar."

Mr. Birnbaum waved Buddy into the shop. He took Buddy under the arm and ushered him into the long, dark wooden storage room behind the shop. It was covered wall to wall, floor to ceiling, with smoked salmon, eel, sturgeon, white fish, and carp —a fragrant mosaic of colors and shapes.

Mr. Birnbaum reviewed his empire with a broad sweep of his right hand, like a king surveying his lands from the castle wall.

"You remember my son, Mark?"

"Sure, Mr. Birnbaum. How is he?"

"Thinks he's a big shot . . . a Wall Street lawyer. Spends fifteen hours a day in a dingy office choked by a tie and stiff white shirt; works harder and gets paid less per hour than I pay a counterman. I said, 'Mark, take over the deli. Be with real people, make a decent living, and spend some time with your family.' He laughed! 'I don't want to schlep boxes and have fish smell all over me all the time. You sent me to law school so I wouldn't have to do that.' Maybe

24

you can talk to him . . . you're a shrewd fellow. You two can be partners."

Buddy put on his most thoughtful look. "I'm up to my eyeballs at the firm, but I'll speak to Mark."

"You kids are schmucks." Mr. Birnbaum shook his head in bafflement. "You get paid by check, have nothing left after taxes. My business is strictly cash, few taxes; all my wealth is hidden in these loxes and sturgeons. Overeducated schmucks work for Uncle Sam . . laugh at real businessmen."

As Buddy left, Mr. Birnbaum called out, "Give your dad my best!"

"Sure will! Thanks. Say hello to Mrs. Birnbaum."

Bud walked down the street toward McGregor's, passing the neighborhood newsstand. Sal Rinaldi put down his *Penthouse* just long enough to ask a question he knew the answer to. "Eating them alive on Wall Street, Buddy boy?"

"Yeah, doing any better would be a sin."

Life was constant in Sunnyside. On a spring day, old folks lined the sidewalks, sitting on their folding chairs, recalling things past, arguing politics, and betting on horse races at the crowded OTB parlor. Youngsters played hit the penny and jumped rope under grandparents' watchful eyes. Teenage boys poured their hearts into stickball, on the same street where Buddy was hit by a car thirteen years ago, while sliding into the sewer cover designated home plate.

Buddy passed the basement where he and Susie

first explored each other. It still pained him to remember their breakup, after four years as high school
sweethearts. Buddy went to Dartmouth, and Susie
commuted to Queens College. After many letters and
a few campus weekends together, Buddy told her,
"We both need space to grow. Let's spend some time
apart."

Susie was helpless to meet the challenge of this
magnificent New England campus and all that it
stood for. She knew Buddy was embarrassed to have
his Queens College girlfriend around and handed him
her gold ankle bracelet, which she had worn every
day since he gave it to her as a freshman in high
school, murmuring softly, "Buddy, you'll be miserable when you get what you think you want."

The streets of Sunnyside suddenly became eerily
empty. Buddy recognized the signal that the World
Championship Soccer Cup match between Ireland
and Italy had started. Everyone simultaneously withdrew to a friend's house or a local bar to watch the
big game. People in Queens enjoyed themselves in
large groups, in contrast to Manhattan where the nu-
clear relationship was the mode.

Buddy pushed open the doors of McGregor's Bar,
to become suddenly immersed in laughter, curses,
and applause, as the ball moved rapidly from foot to
foot. The tube illuminated the otherwise darkened
room, like a lighthouse beacon on a starless night. A
small green, white, and orange flag hung from the
brackets on which the TV rested.

The outline of the well-worn wooden bar, jammed with tall, black leather stools, was etched in the dim light. Buddy moved gracefully over the white floor made of tiny tiles and glided dexterously between packed round tables covered with red-checked table cloths and the ubiquitous pitchers of beer. The room was filled with men and boys of all ages. Several tables played host to three generations, grandfathers, sons, and grandsons. Aside from an occasional slapping of skin or a casual handshake, nobody paid particular attention to Buddy; he was like any other fixture in the establishment. Finally, he arrived at his father's regular wooden booth on the side of the room and slid into it.

Carl Fox was five feet, eight inches tall, with slightly stooped broad shoulders. His brown hair was combed over to the side; his experienced blue eyes showed a man who had lived a full forty-nine years. Carl was the shop steward of his union at Bluestar Airlines. Buddy watched as Carl signed Don Murphy's unemployment slip, encouraging him that better times would come soon.

With that unpleasant task finished, Carl turned his attention to Buddy and gushed forth his anxieties like a pressurized shower head.

"No fun to keep signing these unemployment forms. Fuckin' regulators suspended some of our key routes after that crash last summer. I kept telling them it wasn't faulty maintenance but a defect in the door mechanism ... those greedy manufacturers in Cincinnati!"

"It'll work out, Dad. Just give it some time."

Carl's big fist slammed the tabletop. "Sure, the big-shot bureaucrats in Washington continue to investigate, while working men starve.... You don't look so hot, son. Paper shuffling's giving you bags under your eyes, starting to look old like me."

"Ah, I had a tough day. Some jerk DK'd me and I gotta cover his seven thousand in losses."

"Speak English, will you."

"DK ... said he *didn't know* I bought the options he took a bath in. The fuck lied and reneged on me. Lynch backed him up, nevertheless."

Carl winced. He felt his son's disappointment and humiliation. A dark sadness reflected off Buddy's soul.

"I told you not to go into that racket. All that loose big money attracts the greediest, meanest bastards. With your education, you coulda done anything ... been in charge of making a real product like your brother at Grumman, 'stead of going off and being a salesman."

Buddy bridled at an old pinprick between them. "Look, Dad. I'm not a salesman. How many times I gotta tell you I'm an account executive.

"You get on the phone and ask strangers to put their money in stocks, right? You're a salesman."

"Dad, it takes time. You gotta build a customer base. A reputation. I'm trying to do it. Don't break my balls, too. I already make more money as an account executive than I could as a foreman in some plant."

Both men were deeply unhappy about Buddy's situation, so they vented it on each other.

"I don't get it," exclaimed Carl. "You're always broke. You get thirty-five thousand the first year, fifty grand the next . . . where the hell is it?"

Buddy was on the defensive, because his own upbringing left a residual puzzlement in him as well.

"Fifty K doesn't get you to first base in the Big Apple, Dad, not anymore. I pay forty percent in taxes, thirteen thousand a year in rent; I got school loans, car loans, food; car parking costs me three bills a month, I need good suits at five hundred a pop . . ."

Carl mellowed. He hated to see Buddy seem so vulnerable. "So come home and live rent free, 'stead of in that cockroach palace you live in. Fifty thousand, plus bonuses. Jesus Christ, the world is off its rocker. I made thirty-seven last year . . . brought up three kids on less. And you . . ."

Buddy retorted almost in surrender, a stance that made his father less happy than a strident response would have.

"It's Queens, Dad, and a five percent mortgage, and you rent half the house. I *gotta* live in Manhattan to be a player, Dad. There's no mobility in poverty

29

anymore, y'know. One day, you'll be proud of me."

Carl replied warmly, "I'm already proud of you. It's yourself you've got to be proud of."

Carl recognized that his son's world was spinning beyond both their control. The boy had never known fear before, but without a mooring he was fear's servant. Carl hesitantly tried to lower an anchor. "I ran into Susie the other day. She hasn't seen you in nine months."

"That long already . . . the earth just swallowed me up after the Jackson-Temperance deal."

Carl moved in cautiously. "Why don't you take her to dinner tonight? Her eyes still burn when your name is mentioned."

Buddy longed for familiarity. He rose slightly from his seat, then sank back into the cushion. "I don't have the bread, Dad; especially after today's hit."

McGregor's Bar burst into whoops and applause, as the Irish goalee used his body to make a save against the Italian forward's kick. Carl handed Buddy two crisp $100 bills. "The treat's on me, kid. I always said money is something you need in case you don't die tomorrow."

Buddy squeezed into the tall, dark, wooden phone booth next to the jukebox. He studied the winding pattern of green, orange, yellow, and red stripes on the music box as he dialed Susie's number from ancient memory.

"Hel—"

"Buddy, how are you?" She recognized his voice on the first syllable; Susie had gone over and over this moment so many times in her mind.

"I'm across the street at McGregor's, with my dad. By any chance, are you free for dinner?"

"Buddy, I'd love to see you."

Susie peered out of the third-floor window of her studio apartment, imagining that she could already see Buddy through the darkened TV-illuminated windows of McGregor's Bar.

"How shall I dress? Where are we going?"

"We're going to paint the town. Dinner at Raoul's in SoHo, dancing at Nell's. Like old times, except with new money and Manhattan Island experience."

"I just want to be with you, Buddy. I'll meet you in front of McGregor's."

"Great."

Buddy felt temporarily empowered. His spirit and body connected, like the pleasant tightness of firm muscles after a workout in the gym. Half an hour later, Bud could see her silhouetted in the window of McGregor's Bar. Her red hair and rounded, full smile communicated an inner warmth and optimism.

Bud stood up, shook his father's hand, and not knowing why, practically sprinted out of the bar to her, moving the way a child runs home for lunch. He kissed her, and they walked off talking and laughing, as if an old conversation was taken up without missing a beat.

Raoul's was tout New York. The costumes varied,

as much as the habitués. Shirtsleeves and suits coexisted amicably, while the babble mingled the jargons of art, banking, architecture, movies, law, physics, and advertising. The bar was packed with SoHo singles, generally aspiring to the higher career rungs attained by their older counterparts at the dinner tables.

Rob, the maître d', greeted Buddy and Susie warmly. "Would you enjoy sitting in the garden on such a beautiful evening, Mr. Fox?"

"Love it."

He led them through the front dining area, the large central kitchen with its bustling chefs, sous chefs, and waiters, and into an intimate glass-enclosed dining room surrounded by a backyard urban garden.

"Let's order different entrées, so we can share them," urged Susie.

Bud addressed the waiter. "Escargots and Caesar salad, as appetizers, and soft-shell crab and grilled baby salmon for entrées."

"And from the wine list, Mr. Fox?"

"Robert Mondavi eighty-five, please."

Susie was excited about her new job as editorial assistant with *Archaeological Magazine*.

"I'm editing an article about whether the stone walls and altars that covered miles of Peruvian desert are the work of thousands of Inca Michelangelos or the handicraft of ancient visitors to our planet from outer space."

Buddy experienced a flicker of envy for Susie's

enthusiasm for her work; this quickly turned to admiration for her achievement in rising to the job. Throughout the evening, Buddy was feeling so good about himself, Susie, and New York that he never once mentioned Jackson & Steinhem.

The young couple left on a high after a wonderful dinner. At 11:30 P.M., they grabbed a cab and went to Nell's on West Fourteenth Street. This was the hottest and most fashionable club in town. Admittedly, Buddy had never been there before; however, his browsing in *People* magazine and Chucky Cushing's blow-by-blow descriptions of beautiful people and late nights partying at Nell's had him convinced that this would be paradise revisited.

They emerged from a cab to encounter a crowd six deep, separated from Nell's by a velvet rope enclosure and three muscular bouncers dressed in jet-black cotton T-shirts and skin-tight black jeans tucked into black leather boots. The baby-faced but terribly serious musclemen arbitrarily selected occasional people to cross the cordon sanitaire and enter the black metal doors to Nell's.

Up to a point, the rope was a great leveler, mixing together the fashionable in their designer disco outfits, teenagers in their best from Unique, yuppies trying to demonstrate a relaxed attitude by letting their ties hang loose from open Brooks Brothers' shirt collars, bridge-and-tunnel kids on leave from the boroughs, New Jersey, and Long Island, young men with shaven heads cleaved by Mohawks and girls

33

with punk hairdos as multicolored as the jukebox at McGregor's Bar. Ironically, the bouncers were out-of-work actors, who by day were regularly rejected in auditions by the very same glitzy showbiz types they obsequiously ushered past the eager tryouts pressing for admission to Nell's.

Buddy clutched Susie's hand and pressed forward. At the barrier, he whispered to the guardian. "I'm a friend of Chucky Cushing. He's a member here."

"Are you on the guest list?"

"I think he might have put me down. The name is Fox . . . Bud Fox."

The bouncer made a mechanical sweep of his clip-board. His practical reply was devoid of human timbre. "Sorry, you're not on *the* list."

Buddy reached into his billfold. A crisp $20 bill flashed in his hand. "Look again. I'm sure that Mr. Fox is on *your* list."

The bouncer's eyes were suddenly averted beyond the crowd. A cocoa-colored Rolls Royce, with the initials G.G. etched in gold just below the window, slid up to the curb. The limousine was so finely polished that the shimmering image of the sidewalk crowd reflected perfectly off its side panels. The three bouncers ostentatiously and unnecessarily shoved a two-foot-wide passageway among the on-lookers for their favored guests. A uniformed chauffeur opened the back door as a well-dressed young bodyguard stood pretentiously alert beside the front fender.

A thin, sandy-haired gentleman, about forty-three years old, emerged in a meticulously tailored suit, followed by a beautiful blond girl in a simple flair disco dress, lightly holding on to his outstretched hand. Another GQ couple stepped out behind their host, strutting as if the Red Sea had parted for the foursome. In fact, it had.

Buddy was mesmerized. "That's Gordon Gekko," he whispered to Susie, his eyes never leaving the procession.

Several of the Wall Street yuppies murmured to each other in respectful recognition of Gekko, feared corporate raider and a recent addition to the Forbes 400 list of wealthiest individuals in the United States. Gekko removed the cigar from his mouth and nodded condescendingly to the gaping onlookers. A faint, imperious smile appeared on his closed lips. Getting into Nell's was not enough; part of the pleasure was that others were kept out. Even in business, it was insufficient for Gordon Gekko to win unless there was a clear loser.

Susie tried to soothe what she thought was outrage. "I'm having a great time tonight, Buddy. Let's go home now and be together."

Buddy mumbled. "Gekko's got it all! Money and power, that's all there is."

As they proceeded uptown in a cab, Bud was more motivated than upset. Gekko was on the Ga—Ge list, assigned to him by Jackson & Steinhem.

$ $ $

Before the slam of Bud's apartment door could be heard, he and Susie were fervently kissing in a close embrace. They undressed each other like high school seniors after the prom and slumped to the floor.

Bud wet her soft breasts with his tongue and sucked her pink nipples wet with desire. Susie's pelvis rose slightly to claim her pleasure, as Buddy brushed her clitoris with long, steady strokes. Susie's body felt suspended on the motion alone, as her vagina rounded into a steamy tunnel. She rubbed Buddy's penis in time with her own steady, rhythmic movement and guided him into her. Susie's muscles contracted and held Buddy tight, drawing his body deep within her warm moisture.

They made love so hard that Susie did not notice Bud's vacant stare into the dark space of his bedroom. As he pushed deeper into her, the imperious smile of Gordon Gekko was the burning focus of his imagination.

CHAPTER IV

Gordon Gekko was held fast by the elastic of his memory.

The moon was bright, as the shadowy figures rushed to and fro along the river bank.

"Another sandbag, Gordon . . . higher."

"But the ol' man is gonna take us anyway, Grandpa."

"Someday a flood water *might* cover the cotton fields . . . but you must never stop building the levee higher, Gordon. Pass the sandbag."

"Yes, Grandpa."

"The bigger the dike, the stronger the water needed to knock it down."

Half a continent and three decades away from the tiny rural village of Campsville, Arkansas, along the mighty Mississippi, Gordon Gekko sat in his Wall Street penthouse office looking at the East River and the Statue of Liberty. Gordon's sandbags were now dollar bills, but he could never accumulate enough money to feel secure that he would not drown in the inevitable flood of events. Gekko's apparent greed was actually the unquenchable thirst of fear.

Gekko's childhood was spent in the starkest of rural deprivation. Seasons, floods, and federal farm policies were black and white phenomena, which one observed and rarely judged. Gordon learned to despise dreams and respect the concrete.

The federal government aggressively loaned money to farmers to stimulate production. Surpluses soon depressed farm prices, while government warehouses bulged with subsidized commodities. The government subsidy spigot slowed to a trickle. Then came the drought. The cotton burned in the fields, and mules died by the sides of dusty roads. In the barren countryside, farm families survived on meager produce from their withered vegetable gardens. Unable to meet their loan payments, family farmers such as the Gekkos were forced into foreclosure by the government. Giant corporations from St. Louis and Chicago entered the area to buy the farms under the auctioneers' hammers, at ten cents on the dollar. Politicians and businessmen found good words—"efficiency" and "disciplined production"—to justify the obviously absurd. Gekkos had fought the river and tilled their own soil for five generations. At the rap of a gavel, Gordon's father became a tenant farmer.

Gordon and his pals threw stones at the big-city cars, filled with overweight businessmen on periodic inspection tours of the corporate farms. They walked across the newly turned fields, patting local laborers condescendingly on the back while stepping on freshly planted seeds with their fancy leather shoes.

When Gordon was seventeen, his parents were killed in an automobile accident. He walked to the ferry one morning and crossed the broad Mississippi. Gordon Gekko knew he would never again belong to any one place. He would make the rules, rather than be their victim.

All his possessions were on his body—a flannel shirt, his jeans with the hole at the knee, and a pair of field boots. After days of hitchhiking vaguely east and north, he was picked up by a small real estate operator from Brooklyn. As the miles rolled by, Gekko told his story laconically. Max Sugarman recognized Gordon's iron determination and offered him a job. Three days later he arrived in Brooklyn. Gekko's direction was straight ahead, since there was nothing to go back to.

Gordon's muscular frame and ability to detach action from feeling won him success as a rent collector for Sugarman. He handled the largely black and elderly population in the dilapidated Fort Greene and Park Slope tenements and soon graduated to purchasing such buildings for himself. These neighborhoods became hotbeds of gentrification, and Gekko was a multimillionaire at thirty-five.

Generous gifts to select charities and politicians cleansed Gekko's fortune. The White House had recently referred to "Gekko the Great" in a congratulatory telegram, when he was presented with the "Bootstrap Award."

In 1980, Gekko had applied his considerable fortune and connections to the corporate takeover game. He was bored with real estate. Anyway, financially it was vastly more rewarding and less risky to restructure bloated blue-chips or to intimidate cowardly managements into paying millions of dollars of stockholders' money in greenmail to save their own jobs. Most importantly, he felt that by destroying the corporate bureaucracy's stranglehold on America, he was back on the side of the people. Gordon was no longer a hick kid glancing stones off carpetbaggers' cars. He could score direct hits!

$ $ $

Each day at precisely 2 P.M., Buddy interrupted whatever he was doing to telephone for an appointment with Mr. Gekko. After a month, Gekko's English secretary, Natalie, developed an amused and sympathetic attitude toward the persistent young man with the generic pitch that always ended in rejection.

Marvin Wycoff pointed to the clock. Buddy did deep knee bends to pump up his courage and relieve the tension. "You gotta go for the gold," he steeled himself. Bud buttoned his collar and raised his tie in fetishist acts. As he dialed, Marvin warned him in a paternalistic tone of voice, "Buddy, Buddy, when you gonna realize it's big game hunters that bag the elephants, not rookies. I heard this story about Gekko . . . he was on the phone thirty seconds after the Challenger blew up, selling NASA-related stocks short. He had an ethical bypass at birth."

Buddy leaned forward purposefully into the telephone mouthpiece. "Hello, Natalie—guess who. That's right, and what do you say . . . will you marry me? . . . Then please can you get me through to Mr. Gekko?"

Natalie replied that Mr. Gekko was very busy with a group of Japanese businessmen. Buddy picked right up on the thought. "Of course he's busy, and so am I. Five minutes. That's all I'm asking. There are big changes going on in the international markets. I know that if he could only hear what I have to say, it would change his life."

Natalie was always struck by the personal urgency in Buddy's voice. Indeed, the intensity of his effort had caused her to mention the calls to Gekko. "Mr. Fox, I've told you before, I'm sure you're a good broker, but our traders talk to brokers. Yes, I shall give him your message."

"I love you anyway, Natalie. I'll speak to you tomorrow."

Buddy continued to assemble a comprehensive profile of his prey, while struggling to make contact with him. It was apparent that more than a simple client-moneymaking relationship was at stake, for Buddy Fox had surrendered his soul to a man that he had seen only once. He wanted to crawl under Gekko's skin. Buddy Fox wanted to *be* Gordon Gekko. But how?

CHAPTER V

Buddy's ambition was greater than Gekko's greed. The terms of their engagement had been decided years ago in Campsville and Queens.

Buddy twisted the bolt a thousand ways, trying feverishly to unlock Gekko's door. At last he had a scheme that might work. He stayed awake all night preparing two stock recommendations, using his Apple computer to create spreadsheets that compared operating statistics within their industries; relative price–earnings multiples for similar companies and the S&P 500 index, divisional breakup values, credit coverages, and graphs indicating possible breakouts based on historical price and volume.

The phone rang at 7:45 A.M. It was Carl Fox. "Good morning. You get the cigars I sent you?"

43

"Yeah, Dad, thanks a lot."

"Anytime. Listen, son, I got some great news. Remember that crash last summer? And the investigation?" Carl sounded relieved.

"Sure, Dad."

"Well, the FAA is gonna rule it was a manufacturing flaw in the door-latch mechanism. I kept telling 'em it wasn't maintenance, it was those goddamn greedy manufacturers. And I was right."

"That's great, Dad."

"Damn right. It gets us out from under suspension. We'll get those new routes to Pittsburgh and Boston and the equipment we need. We're gonna compete with the big boys now."

"Hey, to Bluestar Airlines. As your broker, all I can advise is hold on to that stock, Dad."

Buddy's eyes turned to his pile of charts. He reflected for a moment on the news he had just received. "You sure about the FAA findings?"

"Sure . . . I met with them yesterday."

"What about the public announcement?"

"Next week. Some paperwork has to be cleaned up. You okay, Buddy? You sound so distant."

Buddy shook his head, as if emerging from a dream. "Great, Dad. See you soon."

$ $ $

At 1:30 P.M. Buddy asked Dan Hickey to cover his phones. He was going to make a new business call . . . in person. Marvin audited Buddy's best dark blue suit, glanced at the clock, and with a "hmmm," winked at him for good luck.

After a short walk up Broad Street, Fox pushed open the heavy wooden doors engraved with the logo GEKKO & CO. He stood before the receptionist, at the center of a black and white marble floor designed in the shape of a sunburst. He tersely explained his mission. She buzzed Natalie on the intercom.

"It's Daniella. I have a delivery here for Mr. Gekko. A personal item that the gentleman says you have to sign for."

"All right, send him in."

Buddy proceeded nervously down a hallway decorated with exquisite modern art. A Calder mobile twisted in perpetual motion at the end of the corridor. He passed through a small private trading room and entered Natalie's outer office.

"Hello, Natalie, you recognize the voice? I'll give you a hint, you're thinking seriously about marrying me."

Natalie recognized the line. "What are you doing here?"

"I brought a birthday present for Mr. Gekko."

"First of all, Mr. Fox, you can't just come barging in here. And what makes you think it's his birthday?"

Buddy unfolded an old crumpled *Fortune* magazine cover of Gordon Gekko, entitled "Gekko the Great!"

"See! You better go buy him a present. Please, Natalie. Let me give him the gift—Cuban cigars,

Davidoff. I personally saw how much he loves them
. . . and they're hard to get."

Natalie took the gift and told him to stay right
there, while she inquired from Mr. Gekko on his
availability. She returned with a stern look, but with a
note of compromise in her voice. "Wait outside in the
reception room. If he has time during the day, he'll
call you in. . . . Good luck!"

Buddy waited nervously for two hours, alternately
worrying about what Mr. Lynch would do if he observed that Buddy had missed three business hours
and whether he would get to see Mr. Gekko at all.
Despite the air conditioning, Buddy's shirt was
soaked at the armpits with perspiration; his forehead
was shiny from the sweat he kept wiping off his brow
with a wrinkled handkerchief. No matter how stupid
he felt, there was no way he would quit so close to
the starting gate. Suddenly, Natalie stood before him.

"Five minutes."

Buddy readied himself. He focused intently.
"Well . . . life all comes down to a few moments, and
this is one of 'em . . ."

Buddy practically burst into Gekko's office. He
was surprised by its massiveness. The walls were
covered with cherry wood paneling, purchased from
one of the venerable firms that had fallen victim to
the petrodollar interest-rate whipsaw in 1975. Stellas,
Mirós, and Rothkos rested comfortably on the soft,
paneled walls, calling attention to Gekko's complex
character. Fox trembled at the thought that Gekko

might ask him something about the paintings. "Damn, why didn't I take art appreciation at Dartmouth?" he chastised himself, making a mental note to read up on modern art.

The grandeur of the setting did not diminish Gekko, despite his slight stature. His energetic presence electrified everything around him. Dressed in a blue-pinstripe, custom-made English suit, he paced like a caged tiger at the end of a fifty-foot extension cord attached to a blinking gold-plated telephone set. There were no papers on his large early American antique desk. It was, however, weighed down with monitors displaying everything from everywhere— Hong Kong, Tokyo, Frankfurt, London, New York —stocks, treasuries, munis. corporate bonds, gold, commodities, gilts, currencies, mortgages, CDs, ECU . . .

"What the hell is going on?" Gekko's eyes were riveted to the tape, as if his brain were receiving mysterious signals. "I just saw 200,000 shares move. . . . Are we part of it? . . . We better be, pal, or I'm gonna eat your lunch for you."

He punched another line. "Sorry, love it at forty. It's an insult at fifty. What? Their analysts don't know preferred stock from livestock. Wait for it to head south, then we'll raise the sperm count on the deal. . . . Right. Get back to me."

Gekko, pointing to Buddy, fixing dark, intent eyes on him as he still stood frozen at the door, addressed Alex, an aide who listened to his phone conversations while jotting down commitments. "This is the kid who's called me fifty days in a row. Wants to be a player. There oughta be a picture of him in the dictionary under persistence."

Gekko hit a blinking light on the private red phone, not altogether removing his gaze from Buddy. It seemed that the old veteran was about to flash his goods before the young recruit.

"Look, Jerry, I'm looking for negative control, no more than thirty to thirty-five percent, just enough to block anybody else's merger plans and find out from the inside if the books are cooked. If it looks as good as on paper, we're in the kill zone. We lock and load, pal."

He motioned invitingly to Buddy. "Sit down, boy." The soft, almost southern accent betrayed his upbringing. Buddy could not believe that this calm voice belonged to the same person who was just bellowing into the phone.

Gekko himself was no longer sure of who he was. He believed that all men, like himself, were motivated to success by fear. Vanity, lust, prejudice, and greed were the eddies that gave the fear-current variation. He did not discount love and honor but recognized that they were transient emotions, easily changeable in the face of a challenge from survival or ambition.

Gordon adjusted his conduct to act in whatever manner seemed necessary to force others to do his bidding. Love, hate, temptation, submission, aggression, and enticement were equal weapons in his arsenal. He singled out occasions to punish his enemies brutally, and publicly, to discourage others from contemplating an attack on him. Since Gekko never dared to be himself in the world of devils he perceived, pretense became his reality.

Gekko was outwardly one of the most aggressive businessmen of his era; however, years of living had acquainted him with the dangers of impetuous action. He had, after all, much to lose. This was no longer Gekko, the impoverished youth from Campsville, who could seize every opportunity with an intensity reflecting only his hunger to have anything for tomorrow.

At forty-three he was conflicted by his growing conservatism and respectability. Secretly Gordon envied the hot youths who brought him bold deals that represented too much economic or legal risk. Gordon's emotions were his spur, experience his rein. He wanted the impossible—the best of youth combined with the wisdom of age, a desire that might be fulfilled in a mentor relationship. Neither Buddy nor Gordon realized that the hunter and the hunted were really both hunters.

Buddy nervously seized the initiative, before Gekko could grab another call.

"How do you do, Mr. Gekko. I'm Bud Fox. I've read all about you. I think you're an incredible genius. I've always dreamed of only one thing . . . to do business with a man like you."

"Horseshit! I only hope that *you* are intelligent. Like the cigars, how'd you get these?"

"Got a connection at the airport."

"Where are you from, son?"

"Jackson & Steinhem."

"No, who were your parents? Where were you brought up?"

"Queens."

"Good people. You come from Irish stock?"

"Yes."

"Strong . . . but they dream too much. What does your father do?"

"Mechanic." Buddy was afraid to specify aircraft, for fear of compromising his source of the illegal cigars.

"Mechanic. . . . Is he any good?"

"Excellent."

"Rare these days. Great! So, what firm did you say you're with, pal?"

"Jackson & Steinhem."

"Firm's going places, since Temperance dismantled that good-old-boy network . . . has a good junk bond department. You got the financing on that Syndicam deal."

"Yeah, and we're working on some other interesting stuff."

Buddy didn't have a second to relax before Gekko pounced on the opening. "A cosmetics company by any chance? What are you, the twelfth man on the deal team? The last to know?"

Buddy squirmed uncomfortably in his chair but didn't go for the bait. He replied with a knowing smile. "Can't tell you that, Mr. Gekko."

Gordon admired his balls, as well as his evident street smarts. He smelled his ambition and recognized the motivating fear.

"So, whattya got for me, sport? Why are you here?"

Buddy reached into his attaché case and handed Mr. Gekko a pile of charts. "Chart breakout on this one here . . . uh, Whitewood-Young Industries . . . low P.E. Explosive earnings rebound expected, thirty percent discount from book. Great cash flow anticipated. Couple of big holders. Strong management . . ."

Gekko let the pile of charts drop from his hands to the floor, close to Bud's feet.

"It's a dog. What else you got, sport, besides connections at the airport?"

Ollie Steeples, a giant of a man with red suspenders over a protruding potbelly, burst in without knocking, announcing that Stevenson was on the wire from San Francisco. Gekko's face tensed slightly as he picked up the phone.

"He respond to the offer? What! What the hell's Cromwell doing giving lecture tours when his company's losing sixty million a quarter? I guess he's giving lectures on how to lose money. If this guy opened a funeral parlor, no one would die. This turkey is totally brain dead. Well, teatime is over . . . business is business. Dilute the sonofabitch."

Gekko threw out an aside to Bud about Ollie Steeples. "Watch him . . . doesn't look like it, but he's the best trader on the Street. Ya know, genius is having the best subordinates." He buzzed Natalie, who looked surprised to see Buddy still in there. "Get that LBO analysis on Teldar Paper and bring it here." His look at Bud then communicated the command, *what else you got?* Bud was ready.

"Tarafly. Analysts don't like it . . . I do. The breakup value is twice the market price, and the pieces are readily salable. The deal finances itself. Sell off two divisions, keep . . ."

Gekko sneered but shared a coach's look with Alex to indicate a good practice pass.

"Not bad for a technician, but it's a dog with fleas." Gekko looked at his watch, signaling impatience. "Come on, tell me something I don't know. It's my birthday, pal, surprise me."

Gekko glared penetratingly at Bud as he opened a birthday card and fed it into the shredder beside his desk. The soft and menacing sound of the shredder created the proper note of apprehension in Buddy. He got the message — it was fourth down, with one play to go. Gekko built up the pressure by obviously shifting his attention to the Quotron. Bud's anxiety exploded. He rose from his chair, like a mummy being unwrapped, and blurted out: "Bluestar Airlines."

Buddy felt trapped. Beads of perspiration welled on his brow. Gekko sensed the kill. He noticeably relaxed in his chair. His voice was now calm and patient . . . understanding. "Rings a bell somewhere. So what?"

"A comer. Eighty medium-body jets. Three hundred pilots, flies northeast, Canada, some Florida and Caribbean routes . . . great slots in major cities."

Gekko interrupted, now expertly playing Buddy like a fiddle. "Don't like airlines, lousy unions."

Bud tuned in. "There was a crash last year. They just got a favorable ruling on a lawsuit. Even the plaintiffs don't know."

Gordon had achieved virtuoso subtlety, appearing only mildly interested. "How do *you* know?"

Bud's long hesitation indicated his extreme suffering. Gekko believed that men will do almost anything to avoid suffering. He prodded Buddy gently with a "What did you say?"

"I know . . . the decision will clear the way for new planes and route contracts. There's only a small float out there, so you should grab it. Good for a five-point pop."

Buddy had subconsciously prepared for the moment when ambition would overtake honor. It was still very, very hard.

Ollie rushed back in, as excited as he ever got under his rolls of flesh. His voice was deadpan, conspiratorial. "Just got 250,000 shares at eighteen and a quarter from Liberty; think I'll pull twice that at eighteen and a half outta the California pensions. We got close to half a million Teldar shares in the bag."

"Hey, the Terminator! Blow 'em away Ollie."

"*And*, I'm sure we got the Bleezer brothers out of Tulsa coming in with us, and I'm working on the Silverberg boys in Canada."

Before Ollie even finished, Gekko turned his attention abruptly to Buddy. "You got a card, kid?"

Bud thrust a card into his hand. "My home number is on the back . . ."

Gekko glanced at the card. The same imperious smile that he wore when he passed through the crowd at Nell's reappeared on his lips.

"Bud Fox, I look at a hundred ideas a day. I choose one."

Without a word of encouragement or a goodbye, Gekko rose from his desk and strolled to the other end of the massive office. He signaled Alex to show Fox out. Buddy scrambled on the thick oriental carpet to pick up his charts and papers, which Gekko had deposited there without so much as a glance. As he walked through the door, he overheard—Fox could not tell whether it was intentional or accidental —Gekko's strategy for Teldar Paper.

"Okay, gang, looks like we're going over five percent in Teldar Paper. Start the lawyers on a 13D and a draft set of tender documents. Meanwhile, keep buying every share in sight, with a limit of $22. They're gonna fight . . . they got Meyers and Thromberg doing their legal work—they make Nazis look like good guys."

Buddy closed the door behind him. Uncharacteristically, he walked by Natalie without saying a word, and she ignored him.

"Messrs. Jackson and Goldschmidt in Dallas, Kalish in Delaware, and Stevenson in San Francisco are all on hold for a conference call with you, Mr. Gekko," Natalie said into the intercom.

The overwhelming reality deepened Buddy's depression. *A business and moral crisis in my life,* he thought, *is a blip in Gordon Gekko's busy afternoon.*

Buddy returned to his cubicle at Jackson & Steinhem. Marvin inquired, "Well, see him?"

"Yeah, but he didn't see me."

The sales manager painfully dragged his gout-swollen foot by Buddy's cubicle. "Where you been the last three hours, Fox? I wouldn't be sitting around chin wagging if I were you. Plenty of rich men on that computer list who you can cold call . . ."

Marvin gave Lynch the Italian salute behind his back. Buddy did not react. He stared inertly at his Quotron screen. Marvin patted him on the back as his eyes perused Buddy's Quotron. On the otherwise dark screen, bright green symbols leaped out: TLD L 18 1/2, V 1,213,000. Buddy stared pensively, as if deciding on whether to take a weighty action.

Marvin shook him slightly. "Whew. Some volume for Teldar Paper. Did you get a tip from him? Should we be buying?"

Buddy slammed his right index finger on "erase." The screen blackened. He was determined, no matter how much he needed the money, not to suffer another indignity at the hands of Gordon Gekko by buying Teldar.

"No . . . a dog with fleas."

It was pride rather than integrity that caused Buddy to resist temptation. That afternoon Gekko had forced him to explore his darker side. Buddy hated the chilling feeling of personal vulnerability. For the first time, he could emotionally understand fear—why the soldier runs under fire . . . the prisoner squeals on his best friend. G.G. had destroyed this blind youth's false machismo. Fox determined to give Gekko no more of himself.

CHAPTER VI

Anne Darien Taylor judged who she was by whom she was with.

As the daughter of a middle-level advertising executive at J. Walter Thompson, she was raised in the "low-rent" neighborhood of the wealthy Connecticut suburb of Darien. She was very selective about her friends, following with a vengeance her mother's advice that one should befriend only those who "can add something to you." Despite the fact that her family was hardly la crème de Darien, by the time Anne was a teenager, she had affected every mannerism of upper-class suburban life. Anne was so prototypical of the WASP suburban debutante that she lost her real name in boarding school and was forever known by her middle name, Darien.

Darien relished being an interior decorator, although she was in it neither for the money nor for a love of furniture. Darien was a collector of beautiful people. Interior decorating was her vehicle to the glamorous and rich. Her considerable progress was chronicled in both *House and Garden* and *Town and Country,* although she still largely served the up-and-coming set that Mark Hampton did not have time for.

Darien's biggest coup thus far was landing Mr. Gordon Gekko as a client. When she paraded this accomplishment before her now-retired father, he responded with, "Who's that?" Darien admonished him for his ignorance in not having heard of "Gekko the Great."

George Taylor laughed. "Bet you couldn't name even one emperor of the Han dynasty . . . and they wielded absolute power." Darien was neither amused nor enlightened by George's historical perspective.

$ \qquad $ $ \qquad $ $

Buddy did not notice Darien when he entered Ernie's, a trendy yuppie bar on Broadway. After a thoroughly disheartening day, he had decided to forego his nightly bout with the charts and computers.

The huge wooden bar at Ernie's was packed four deep. Tight clusters of affluent-looking young professionals, drinks in hand, filled in the spaces around the rest of the room. Others sat at tables peppered with tall colorful drinks that seemed to match Ernie's emphasis on presentation: margaritas, piña coladas, daiquiris. If generations are defined by their drinks, this was no simple scotch-on-the-rocks era.

Perhaps the most shocking thing to the boys at McGregor's Bar, just four miles and many generations away from the Upper West Side, would be the yuppie fad of drinking very light Mexican beers with a twist of lime squeezed in the bottle for flavor.

The singles bars created a tribal scene—costumes, rituals, status. The anonymity and pressures of the work day, in this most populous and gregarious city, left these young men and women with a desperate hunger for human contact. Crowds of similar people engaged in ritualistic interaction provided this generation with its temples.

These were the yuppies whose skills and energies supported the service industries and reclaimed whole neighborhoods, bringing their own culture with them: fast food, boutiques, clubs, bookstores, and all-night grocery stores—with premium everything, from soup to soap.

Ernie's was an extension of both home and office. It provided a locus for matchmaking, or just plain sex, as well as a useful forum for networking. Money was something unashamedly on everybody's mind and tongue. "Striver" used to be a put-down: At Ernie's, one would ask if there was anything else that one should strive to be.

Yuppies swapped stories of rapid rises and dismal falls. If the stories were apocryphal, they illustrated the point nevertheless; if they were true, so much the better. Buddy hardly had to eavesdrop to overhear an animated tale about an allegedly wildly successful dealmaker . . .

"You know Marty Wyndham. He netted $650,000 out of that merger. . . . Twenty-six years old, the guy's a Rambo. Got himself a Porsche Turbo Cabriolet, about seventy-five thou, got a house in Westhampton, penthouse on Second Avenue, gets up at two-thirty in the morning, he's in the office at four . . . guy never sleeps. . . . He's Rambo, man . . ."

Such stories made Buddy feel that that he was slipping down a greasy career pole in comparison with his peers. He ordered another margarita, hoping to dull his senses to the constant chatter about money and deals around him. Like a lion surveying a zebra herd at midday, Buddy shifted his eyes lazily around the room, as if not expecting too much for his effort.

Somewhat removed from the crowd, Darien was leaning against a white post with a pale yellow lamp reflecting light from just above her. Darien's aloof beauty against the plain background added to her magnificence.

Buddy's eyes bonded to her like a laser beam. It was hard for him to imagine what such a refined beauty was doing in a singles bar—alone. From her pose, he could not know that Darien was waiting for her date. Darien was a fisherman: She could not help dangling a line whenever near water with the general optimism that something unpredictably wonderful might bite.

For the second time in a few hours, Buddy stoked his courage. Despite his fatigue, he approached her, because he could not do otherwise.

"Hi . . . can I buy you a drink?"

"Please, no thanks!" It was clear from her disdainful look that this was not the fish she hoped to catch.

"Look, I know you get approached a lot by aggressive men, but I'm different. I rarely talk to strangers. All my life I've been waiting for the right person to walk across the room. You're that person; you don't know it but I do. If you walk off now, I'll never see you again or you me. You'll grow old."

"Oh, really." Darien smiled in gentle amusement, as he continued.

"I'll grow old. We'll both die. And we'll never have known each other. I could swear I've seen you before . . . and lost you. That's sad. At least one drink for a dreamer. What's your favorite drink?"

Darien looked at him, somewhat unsure. His looks were attractive, but was he serious or glib?

"Okay, Grand Marnier."

"Don't go away."

His eyes reflected the blarney in him—was all his bad luck just preparation for this great luck? Bud pushed through the crowd and captured the bartender's attention. Meanwhile, a handsome, wealthy-looking man about thirty-five years old kissed Darien on the cheek and led her out of Ernie's. Buddy was stung as the woman of his dreams disappeared out the door, without so much as a backward glance. The bartender repeated his question.

"What do you want?"

"I just lost it . . ."

CHAPTER VII

Bud's internal turbulence intruded on his world at Jackson & Steinhem. Hy Lynch was riding Buddy harder as the pressures on sales management mounted. A steady stream of top commission producers flowed out of the sales department, as "managers" assumed much of the authority and prestige that used to belong to the money-makers. They went to boutique firms, or even to other financial supermarkets, where the memory of better days was not so painful. The bureaucrats responded by screwing the place down harder, imposing quotas on every department and on each salesman. The plan was to identify and eliminate the bottom fifteen percent, whom they considered to be occupying valuable space unproductively. In the not-too-distant future, with the top and bottom gone, Jackson & Steinhem would become a firm of steady midlevel men, very much like its insurance company parent, Temperance.

Hy Lynch spoke to Lou Manheim about Buddy's declining production. Lou was aware of Buddy's feelings about the changes that had occurred since the merger when he called him to his desk. Indeed he shared some of Fox's reservations and nostalgia.

"Hy tells me you've missed your quota. Anything wrong . . . that I can be of help with?"

"I'm making the same effort as before, Mr. Manheim . . . just not getting the same result. Bad streak of luck . . . I guess."

"Buddy, you're not selling pots and pans here, you're selling trust and confidence . . . a set of intangibles. If you don't believe in the institution, you can't sell it to others. It's like a jungle out there. If you're wounded, the animals sense it. They lose confidence and move away—or worse . . . go for you."

Buddy nodded in resignation, as Mr. Manheim went on.

"Even if the institution is not what you signed on for, it can still offer a lot to you, both professionally and personally. Maybe the changes are good . . . at least necessary. We need more structure and management now that we're so big and operating in such a competitive arena. You must adjust to survive!"

Buddy interrupted. "I'll try, Mr. Manheim . . . I'll try."

"If you mix up fantasy with reality, you'll be paralyzed."

"Thank you, sir. I understand, sir."

$ $ $

The firm's jungle drums sent out the message that Buddy was in trouble. Chuck Cushing immediately distanced himself. Cushing knew that he was also under scrutiny by Temperance management, as part of the old-boy network. They found him alien, his methods different, even though he was a big producer.

Bud felt increasingly isolated, except for the constancy of his relationships with Marvin Wycoff and Dan Hickey. The young sales assistants looked at Buddy differently now that the word was out. The reverence accorded to him as a favorite of the old regime—coattails they could ride—vanished. Now he was an obstacle in their ascent to account executive—they wanted his cubicle.

Buddy's despondency was interrupted by a shout from Gina, the pool secretary. "Call for you, Buddy."

He picked up the phone in a desultory fashion but reared up in his seat so abruptly that Marvin couldn't help staring at him in anticipation of either great or horrible news. At the other end Gordon Gekko leaned back in his chair to get a better view of the Statue of Liberty while talking into his speakerphone.

"All right, Bud Fox . . . buy me twenty thousand shares of Bluestar. No more than fifteen and an eighth, three-eighths tops, and don't screw it up, sport."

"Yes, sir. Thank you. You won't regret it."

Bud always said the purpose of the game was to win by its rules. Suddenly, he was satisfied just to win.

Marvin approached Buddy as if he was a high school senior opening a college acceptance letter.

"Uh . . . got a little action there, eh, Buddy?"

"Marv . . . I just bagged the elephant."

$ \qquad $ \qquad $

A few days later a cluster of brokers and sales assistants were huddled around Buddy's cubicle, prior to the opening bell. Word had spread about Buddy's landing of Gekko the Great with a cold call, and the latter's purchase of Bluestar Airlines. At 9:15 A.M., a Reuters dispatch had come across the screen.

FAA lifts Bluestar suspension. Approves new routes. Opening in the stock delayed due to an imbalance of orders.

Buddy called the head equity trader for an indication of where the specialist might open the stock. "Nineteen. Thanks, Sidney."

Dan Hickey was genuinely excited for Buddy, being somewhat acquainted with the empty feeling of being at the bottom of the barrel. "The man of the day. Pour some water on him to cool him off. One of these days I want to know the real skinny on how you got Gekko's account."

"My magic tie, Dan," Bud said, flipping the end of his tie in the air.

"I'll trade you."

Lou Manheim came by to congratulate Buddy. "I knew you'd get it together, Bud. That Bluestar is a good little company. I remember when we got the money for it to buy those first planes, back in the fifties."

A beautiful Chinese sales assistant passed, stopping seductively to ask a question from the instantly created authority.

"Marv said you might like Teldar, Buddy."

"Sleep with me and the secrets of the West are yours," he responded with a caress and smile.

Manheim intervened. "Now that's a crap company. Sure you might make money on the takeover rumors, but you're gambling. What's the company generating? Nothing. No substance to it."

Buddy was feeling good about himself, after a long drought from such positive feelings. In fact, he was a little giddy with relief.

"Old values, Mr. Manheim. Buy it, Julie," he said with a mischievous smile.

Lou Manheim shook his head, almost involuntarily, as he walked off.

When the huddle cleared at the opening, Marv swiveled his chair next to Buddy, a disappointed and agitated look on his face.

"Buddy, Buddy—some buddy; why didn't you tell me to buy Bluestar?"

Fox motioned to Marvin to pipe down and whispered, "Gekko demanded confidentiality."

"Gimme a break. Your client buys Bluestar Airlines Tuesday. Today they just happen to get good news, and the stock goes batshit. He must have ESP. A real Nostradamus. Jesus Christ, what are friends for?"

"All right, I owe you one, Marv."

"That's right, next time a little birdie talks to you, talk to me too, E.F. Hutton."

"Buddy, pick up six. Natalie from Gordon Gekko's office," shouted Gina in an affected English accent.

"Hi, Natalie . . . lunch at 21? Tell Mr. Gekko I'm out the door."

As Bud raced for the door, he bumped into Hy Lynch, who tapped him warmly on the shoulder with the bull's head of his cane. "Nice piece of work, Fox. Why don't you join me in the partners' dining room for lunch tomorrow?"

"I'd love to, Mr. Lynch, thank you."

The last few days had produced dynamite sales from all of Bud's institutional accounts. Buddy was up—way up—and it was infectious with the firm's customers, just as Mr. Manheim had predicted.

CHAPTER VIII

A favorite pastime among diners at 21 Club was to comment on its boring and overpriced food. Nevertheless, some of the wealthiest, most powerful, and even cuisine-oriented New Yorkers daily claimed their respective "regular" tables for lunch in the 21 Grill Room. Like Saratoga, Newport, and Wimbledon, 21 was an institution that served needs well beyond its ostensible purpose.

The patrons were generally people who had risen through the labyrinthine worlds of corporate and political America. The Grill Room was overflowing with CEOs, senior partners, former cabinet members, and an occasional Mafioso, sharing in common the "10" they had achieved in their respective walks of life.

The owners greeted guests by name as they entered the magnificent foyer decorated with perhaps the best private collection of Remington paintings. Indeed, if one was unfortunate enough not to be known by name, he was made to feel that he had not yet earned such recognition. Sometimes, a gentleman would dine with a pretty young woman whom he would casually introduce without a surname, such as "my niece, Joanna" or "my friend, Tamara."

The patrons were distinctly middle-aged and rich. These were people who spent fortunes on designer clothes, in order to appear as if they were not designed at all. The Grill Room ceiling was covered with authentic model trains, antique dolls, brass goblets, and hundreds of other rare memorabilia. 21 Club was a place where people were supposed to have quiet fun, to be pampered with others like themselves. An overabundance of tuxedoed waiters unobtrusively catered to the patrons' every whim. Indeed, an element of the chic was an inconspicuous overabundance of everything.

Almost all of the dining room conversation was about business or power . . . usually both. People ever so briefly stopped by each others' tables for a handshake and perhaps a subtle reminder of an unreturned phone call or a succinctly phrased question about closing a deal.

Gordon Gekko was already seated at his regular table in the inner circle of the Grill Room when Fox was escorted in to join him for lunch. He arrived out of breath.

G.G. recoiled ever so slightly, then broke into a receptive smile when Buddy enthusiastically greeted him with a close-up frontal approach and a broad spread-finger handshake.

"Hi, sport, sit down."

Bud spoke in an anxious tone, mixed with gratitude. "Nice to see you again, Mr. Gekko."

Exercising the tone of a teacher, as well as indicating who was in command, Gekko tried to communicate to Buddy that everything was under control and he should relax.

"Try the steak tartare. It's off the menu, but Louis'll make it for you."

"Of course, sir. And what will the gentleman have to drink?" Bud hadn't even seen the waiter who had followed him to the table.

Buddy searched his mind for something that would be acceptable at 21, as his eye caught a glimpse of bottled water on the next table.

"Uh . . . just Perrier, thank you."

"Would Saratoga be satisfactory for the gentleman?" signaling that this was the brand available.

"Sure . . . Saratoga . . . that's fine."

While he waited to be served, Gekko toyed with a three by six color television. Suddenly he flipped the channel to receive the Dow-Jones averages, with a how's-our-business-doing smile on his face. Bud eagerly picked up on his cue.

"Bluestar was twenty-one and an eighth when I left the office. Might spin up a little more by the bell."

Gekko's tiny smile of satisfaction over Bluestar changed to one of "I gotcha" when he asked, "Teldar's shooting up. Buy any for yourself? Bet you were on the phone two minutes after you got out of my office."

"No, sir, that would have been illegal," he responded somewhat defensively.

Gekko gave him a knowing shoulder pat, to indicate he didn't believe him. "Sure . . . relax, sport. No one's going to blow a whistle. Here, is this legal? You wanna put it in my account? You invest it for me."

Buddy picked Gekko's check off his plate. He gaped at it. The gentleman next to him surreptitiously cocked his head to the side so his eye caught the figure of $1,000,000 on the check. He leaned the other way and whispered to his wife about the odd duo next to them, "You won't believe this, but . . ."

Abruptly, Gekko called to the busboy. "Can I have the bill over here, for Christ's sake."

"Yes, sir!"

Gekko turned on Buddy with the icy hardness of a stalactite. "Cover the Bluestar buy and put a couple hundred thousand in one of those bowwow stocks you mentioned. Use a stop-loss order, to protect your downside. For Christ's sake, buy yourself a decent suit. Go to Morty Sills, tell 'em I sent you."

Buddy was made to feel as low as a crawler by his

mentor's harsh appraisal. G.G. captured the opportunity to give another lesson, "Kid, every day you're evaluated and reevaluated. Life's a blank sheet of paper."

He was confused between the wicked personal assessment and the confidence displayed by Gekko the Great in opening a $1 million personal account with Bud Fox.

"Mr. Gekko—*thank you* for the chance. You won't regret this; you're with a winner!"

G.G. responded icily. "Put the rest of it in a money-market fund account for now. I want to see what you know before I let you invest it . . . and save the cheap salesman talk, it's obvious."

Gekko rose to leave, as Bud looked on in puzzlement. He leaned his head next to Bud's ear and whispered, in a tone so sharp as to pierce Buddy's soul, as he squeezed Fox's arm like a Sicilian don instructing a capo, "You heard me . . . I don't like losses, sport. Nothing ruins my day more than losses. You do good, you get perks, all kinds of perks. Stay home tonight. Louis, take care of 'im. Enjoy the lunch."

Gekko rapidly initialed the check for his 21 house account. A broad, warm smile emerged like a sunrise on his face. "So long, sport," he said as he slowly made his way out of 21 pumping extended hands in every direction.

Bud sat entranced, staring at the million dollar check like a kid who just received his first allowance. The waiter placed the steak tartare with a raw egg on top in front of him. Without eating, Fox rose and walked out of the Grill Room with Gekko the Great's check still clutched in his hand.

Gordon need not have reminded Bud to stay home tonight. He was determined to identify winners for G.G.'s portfolio. Value-Line Reports, Granville contrarian analyses, and flash research updates were strewn across the apartment. A half-eaten cold pizza lay on the wooden bridge table that served as Fox's dining room.

Bud did not expect any visitors when the doorbell rang. In the doorway was a smashing blonde, looking supernatural in a fitted, black Chanel suit, with a tight skirt clinging just below her thighs. Ropes of gold chains decorated her neckline. Her body moved so perfectly when she entered Bud's apartment that it was clear this was one of nature's favored creatures. She was also obviously well cared for. In the context of Bud's apartment, here was a magnificent butterfly among weeds; however, she disguised her disgust well.

"Hello, Buddy, I'm Lisa . . . a friend of Gordo's." Her teasing smile communicated a laid-back California attitude, while the thin ends of her lips curved slightly upward in a subtle promise of more to come.

"Lisa. Gordo? Oh, Mr. Gekko." He shook off his numbers and graphs, beginning to concentrate on what was in front of him. "Would you, uh, like to sit down?" he said, pulling over a wooden frame chair from behind the bridge table.

She looked around the apartment and knew she wanted to get out of it quickly. With a hapless sigh, Lisa rubbed his shoulders. "Oh, that's just like Gordo, not telling you. Get dressed. We're going out."

"We are?"

A stretch limo was in front of the townhouse. Two winos examined it from a respectful distance, not wishing to challenge the oversized chauffeur. When Buddy and Lisa emerged, the winos poked each other in the ribs, howling with delight and heralding Bud's good luck with applause. Fox took a deep bow from the waist and waved majestically to his courtiers. He sneaked a gaze out of the black-tinted limo windows as they pulled away, wanting to see his apartment from this exalted perspective.

"Where are we going?"

"Anywhere you wish, but I strongly suggest you leave it to me." Lisa hiked her skirt midthigh, to acquaint him with the perfection that might be attained.

"John, drive around Central Park for a while." She sealed the panel between them and the driver and turned to Buddy.

Lisa emptied a small plastic bag of white powder into a narrow vial. She drew it into her nose with a deep breath and prepared an offering for Buddy. His hesitation signaled that he had never tried cocaine. Lisa giggled, loosening his tie and unbuttoning his shirt, seductively, slightly out of control.

"Lighten up, Buddy boy . . . let go . . . leave everything to me and enjoy it. Try the blow . . . you'll love it."

After years of watch duty, the abstract notion of lightening up and ceding all responsibility to someone else was more enticing than Lisa could possibly understand . . . but perhaps not Gordon Gekko. However, Buddy had been surrendering his values so liberally these days that he fought to hold on to some touchstone of his identity. He awkwardly surveyed the situation . . . as his nature succumbed to desire. Buddy snorted and felt the rush to his brain.

Lisa unzipped his fly in a swift, experienced movement. She softly stroked up his capability. He was hungry for her, dependent on Lisa for relief. She whispered, "now me," and climbed onto the saddle, like a lance corporal enthusiastically pursuing the infidel. Buddy's whole body rejoiced in the freedom— it was wonderful to surrender everything to Lisa, nothing required . . . like an infant receiving everything, incapable of giving anything in return . . . with nothing expected.

Lisa rocked easily backward and forward, slowly drawing Buddy along her pathways. She turned around on him without losing a beat, rubbing his thighs and scrotum with sweeping rhythmic movements. Lisa tightly gripped his hardness between her soft moist walls, his trembling body seemingly rising against gravity as he streamed deep within the center of her body. Buddy was alone, weightless in space. When he emerged from nirvana, Lisa was gently hugging his parts with a cool, wet towel.

"Would you like anything else?"

"A subscription, please."

"Speak to Gordo . . . he's my publisher."

The limousine dropped Buddy off at his doorstep. Forty-five minutes later, Gordon was on the phone.

"How'd you like Lisa?"

"Unbelievable, Mr. Gekko, fireworks!"

"Beats all this free-love shit. A thousand bucks, but expertise counts! When I was your age I was trading one-month rent extensions for blow jobs in tenement hallways. You got the world by the tail, kid, enjoy it."

Click . . . Gordon hung up.

Lisa had eradicated Buddy's physical hunger, but his spiritual tundra remained.

CHAPTER IX

Gordon felt that his natural and acquired gifts were being squandered on the same challenges that he had successfully conquered a decade ago. He yearned to see things with the fresh eyes of youth . . . but he recognized that exposure to the new meant encountering hazards that could destroy the old. The raider inwardly struggled with his ambivalence while maintaining the business-as-usual posture expected of Gekko the Great by his perceived audience.

Gekko liked Buddy, because he wanted *it* so much. However, he didn't trust him, because his education and bourgeois upbringing had produced a dangerously soft underbelly. In crisis, the only time it counted, such a young man might choose the simple pleasures and familiarity of peace, rather than the rigors of war. Gekko's innate shrewdness warned him against any association with Fox, while his spiritual desires made him press the relationship further.

$ $ $

Gordon and Bud played squash at the Athletic Club, a late-Victorian stone monument, built with a splendor proscribed thereafter by the minimum wage. Gekko loved to plunder his protégé's youth as he artfully moved him around the court.

"Come on, sport, you gotta try harder. I need some exercise, for Christ's sake."

"Gordon, I don't think I can . . . go on."

"Finish out the game, Bud, push yourself . . ."

Gekko maneuvered the ball just beyond Buddy's easy reach, but close enough for him to go for it . . . center . . . back wall . . . right wall . . . left wall . . . Buddy played every point, until breathless, he smashed into the wall and collapsed like a panting puppy dog. After seeing Buddy was not hurt, Gekko laughed triumphantly as he hauled Buddy off the floor.

"You gotta learn to take control of the ball, Buddy. And stamina—most games are won with persistence. Read Sun Tzu's *The Art of War*. Every battle is won before it is ever fought. Think about it."

As Gordon entered the steam room, everyone tried to gracefully reposition himself closer to him, to talk of deals, a favorite charity, or just to be able to tell the little lady that he had chatted with Gekko the Great at the club today.

"Nice club, Gordon."

"Yeah . . . I came to New York with a flannel shirt, hole in my dungarees, and a pair of field boots. Nobody gave me a break, except for Max Sugarman . . . rest his soul. Now that I don't need 'em, these Ivy League schmucks are sucking up to me. Remember, you're alone, pal . . . all alone."

Buddy decided to break the bad news, while Gordon was in such a mellow mood.

"Uh, Mr. Gekko, we took a little loss. We got stopped out on Teleco . . . about a hundred thou."

"Why didn't you tell me before, when we could have done something about it?"

"I thought it would come back. We just invested a little too soon."

"Yes."

Gekko's mood darkened. He hated amateurs who didn't understand that the best loss was the first loss, held on into oblivion. This was not $100,000—could have been $100 million—it was principle.

"To be right too soon is to be wrong, sport."

"But . . . Mr. Gekko, I studied the fundamentals. I . . . I—"

Gekko angrily interrupted. "You're not as smart as I thought you were. Buddy boy, listen hard. Don't count on Graham and Dodd to make you a fortune. Everybody in the market knows the same theory! Most of these high-paid MBAs don't make it. You need a system—discipline. The ball is pitched across the plate every day. Don't swing at the fast balls, the screwballs, the curve balls . . . wait for a nice, fat, slow ball right across the plate . . . drive it out of the ball park. You just need one, so never be in a hurry. And if you make a mistake, never fall in love with it, never hide it. Take your loss. *No feelings!* You don't win 'em all, you don't lose 'em all, you keep on fighting. If you need a friend, get a dog; it's trench warfare out there, sport . . . and in here, too. I got twenty other brokers out there analyzing charts. I don't need another one. Talk to you sometime."

Buddy was panicking. He had submitted himself to an absolute master and was being read out of the party.

"I'm not another broker, Mr. Gekko. One more chance, *please!*"

Gekko despised such shows of weakness. Could he ever make Fox combat-hardened?

"I don't want a broker, Fox. I need a businessman. Someone who doesn't put us at the mercy of events —someone who helps create events that work *for* us. Dammit, get dressed. We'll see, once and for all, if you have what it takes."

The two entered Gekko's limousine and cruised up Park Avenue. Gordon slid open a wooden panel to reveal an IBM PC and punched in the name Laurence Wildman. His complete background, plus a summary of his five percent or more stock positions, appeared on the screen.

"Know the name?"

"Course. Larry Wildman was one of the first raiders."

Gekko's face became intense, his eyes indicating a cold-blooded mission to be performed.

"*Sir* Larry Wildman. Like all Brits, he thinks he was born with a better pot to piss in . . . bribed an old secretary of mine to open her mouth and stole RDL Pharmaceuticals right out from under me. Wildman, the white knight . . . word's out that he suckered me. He must be punished—publicly—or every sharp-shooter in town will be taking aim at me."

Buddy sat wide-eyed, a school girl learning about her best friend's love affair. "I remember that deal."

Gekko delivered the old Sicilian saw: "Revenge is a dish best served cold. I've wanted . . . well, it's payback time. Wildman just became an American citizen. My mole tells me something big is about to come down. I have half the picture. I want to know where he goes and who he sees. I want *you*, sport, to give me the missing half of the picture."

Bud's palms were cold with anxiety. "Follow him? Mr. Gekko, I . . . It's not what I do. I could lose my license if the SEC found out. It's inside information, isn't it?"

Gekko was disgusted. Had he been taken in by a wimp, who only appeared to have brass balls?

"Inside information. Oh, you mean like when a *father* tells his son about a court ruling on an *airline*? Or someone overhears me saying I'm gonna buy Teldar Paper? Or the chairman of the board of XYZ suddenly knows it's time to blow out XYZ? You mean that?"

Bud stared in disbelief. "You know about my father?"

Gekko smirked. "The most valuable commodity I know of is information. Are we in agreement?"

Gekko felt the rage of a thwarted father. He kept seeing visions of tenants putting guns to his head when he collected rents in Brooklyn, being left for dead by thugs in an alleyway, risking everything. This whimpering Harvard MBA asshole wanted it all . . . and didn't have the balls to take it. A venomous darkness spewed forth a brew of disappointment and hatred.

"I'm afraid, sport, unless your father is a union representative of another company, you and I are gonna have a hard time doing any business," he said jeeringly.

Buddy retreated to the sophomoric. "What about hard work?"

Gekko was so revolted by the cantaloupe pulp he was poking that he abandoned his own maxim of nothing personal.

"What about it? You work hard. I'll bet you stayed up all night analyzing that dog you bought. And where'd it get you? My father and mother worked hard, too! Like elephants—paid the bills, law-abiding suckers. The bank, the corporations—yeah, the government of the U.S. of A.—all conspired to steal their farm, all 'legal,' of course. *Wake up, pal.* If you're not inside, you're *outside.*"

Buddy murmured weakly, "I'm really sorry . . . really sorry about your folks."

Gekko flushed a bit with unaccustomed embarrassment and quickly recovered his measured tone. "I'm not talking about a $200,000-a-year, working Wall Street stiff, flying first class and being comfortable. I'm offering you *rich,* pal, rich enough to fly your own jet, rich enough not to *waste time*—or *nothing.* You had what it takes to get through my door. Next question: You got what it takes to stay?"

Gekko pressed the button to roll down his side window as they passed the Sixty-seventh Street Armory shelter for the homeless. A richly dressed executive waited to cross Park Avenue, while next to him a bum rummaged for food in the wire garbage can on the corner.

"You really think the difference 'tween this guy and that guy is luck? White House says don't feed the starving man 'cause you might ruin his philosophical attitude toward hard work. Look, pal, you *don't* think it's hard work to seek your three squares a day in the garbage can?"

Buddy was washed out. A boy, his vapid clichés perhaps even halfheartedly said, stomped under the boot of Gekko's reality, too inexperienced to summon forth any different reality of his own.

"Mohammed, pull over. . . . When it comes to money, sport, everybody's of the same religion. Or should be. . . . Hope you don't mind if I let you off here, I'm late for a meeting. . . . Goodbye, nice knowing you."

It was hard to tell where business ended and personal elements began. Gekko turned his head away and reached for his sedative, the telephone. Fox got out, pursed his lips like a little boy about to get even, and tapped on the smoked glass window.

"All right, Mr. Gekko . . . you got me."

Gordon placed the receiver in the mounting. A wary look crossed his face, melting into a fatherly contentment—his son had seen the light.

"Yeah, it's a beautiful night. I love this hot, stinkin' city . . . nothing else like it in the world. Seven million people living on each other's heads, kids born, millionaires dying, people praying, junkies, whores, wills, lawyers, deals, parties, sex . . . guys like you, sport—dreaming about New York is everything you can do here. And the worst thing is everything you *can't* do here."

Gekko shut the limo door and drove off. Buddy stood rigidly on Park Avenue, between the armory and the Harold Pratt mansion. A granite look of anticipation marked Bud as he walked up Park Avenue. Gekko's mallet and chisel had liberated Fox's ambition from its stone.

CHAPTER X

Sir Laurence Wildman cultivated respectability as a fundamental part of his business strategy. Modernization of Britain's moribund textile industry, as well as assistance to one of the Queen's daughters who found herself in an embarrassing personal situation, earned a peerage for Larry Wildman. This gave him the respectability to get the credit he needed to expand his empire.

Wildman was a master of the bear hug. Byron Metz, his publicist, emphasized ad nauseam that *Sir* Laurence never engaged in hostile transactions. He had a set modus operandi. Wildman accumulated at least ten percent of the outstanding shares in an undervalued corporation and worked hard to ingratiate himself with management as a "stabilizing" shareholder, who would protect the company from sharks like Gekko. He learned about these companies from the inside while continuing slowly to buy more shares. Then he'd make a bid jointly with management, for whom he arranged financing to buy its own stake in the company. As a result of this soft-sell procedure, which keyed off both the fear and the greed of management, Sir Laurence was able to control large corporations without paying the normal fifty to one hundred percent premiums that accompanied outright hostile bids. Some critics suggested that everybody gained by this civilized approach, except the shareholders who sold to Sir Larry without receiving their control premium.

Wildman was considered arrogant by many, since his intense concentration caused him to ignore anything that was not of central interest to him. Such indifference was apparent as he climbed into his Bentley at 9:00 A.M. in front of his apartment at 835 Fifth Avenue without so much as a good morning or nod to the doorman and personal assistants who cordially greeted him. He certainly paid no attention to the helmeted rider on a Kawasaki 500 motorcycle, which pulled around the corner to follow him through the jammed streets of New York City.

Bud parked the motorcycle and rushed through the lobby of 55 Water Street, barely catching up to the Wildman party in the elevator. They exited on the thirtieth floor reception area of Ruff & Co., one of the cleverest and most aggressive investment banks on Wall Street. Bud followed them out of the elevator and stood nearby in his helmet, the patient messenger waiting for a pickup. Sir Laurence was familiarly greeted by Duke Friedman, kingpin equity trader on the Street. Buddy retreated and waited by the newsstand in the lobby for two hours, until Wildman emerged.

Buddy followed the Bentley to One New York Plaza where, after a brief interval, Wildman came out of the building with Arthur Milcus of Feldman, Samuels, Sachs & Harman, leading SEC attorneys specializing in mergers and acquisitions. They raced to the American Bank & Trust Company headquarters at 280 Park Avenue. Bud followed them into the sparsely appointed lobby but was stiffly rebuffed by a guard when he produced neither an identification badge nor a visitor's pass. At 2:15 P.M., Wildman emerged on the sidewalk, arm in arm with Greer Gorham, after an obviously successful luncheon in the chairman's private dining room. Several well-attired bank officers waved warmly to Wildman's party as the Bentley pulled away from the curb.

The Kawasaki sped several cars behind the Bentley on the Long Island Expressway to the Marine Aviation Terminal exit. Bud felt like an urban terrorist, coldly efficient and ruthless in carrying out his deadly mission.

The Bentley barreled along the access road past La Guardia's commercial airlines and zipped onto the field at Butler Aviation, pulling alongside a waiting

Wildman Industries Gulfstream. The jet taxied down the runway, leaving Buddy to suck its exhaust, with his face and palms pressed against the fence. His bewilderment galvanized into a hasty plan of action when his eye caught the flight mechanic turning toward the terminal.

Bud raced onto the field. "Oh shit, don't tell me Mr. Wildman was on board that plane."

The mechanic nodded.

"My boss will *kill* me. I was supposed to give him this"—waving his black notebook—"to brief him for an important meeting. You know where that plane is going?"

"Erie, Pennsylvania." The mechanic walked back to Butler, with Buddy close behind him in search of a pay phone. Bud proudly called his mentor.

". . . after spending the morning at Ruff & Co. with Duke Friedman, senior equity trader, he had lunch at American Bank & Trust Company . . . with the chairman. . . . I'd say from all of the arm-waving and sweet smiling on the sidewalk after lunch, Larry arranged some nice, fat financing, G.G. His plane took off for Erie, Pennsylvania."

Gekko punched Anacott Steel up on his screen. His eyes brightened when he observed that the price of ANC had not moved from 45½.

"So, what's the bottom line, sport?" After a pause, Gordon decided to play with Buddy a little, while teaching him to draw concrete conclusions. "Bright, but not bright enough, Sherlock; roll the dice and play a little Monopoly. . . . What box would be big enough for Sir Laurence to land on in Erie, Pennsylvania?"

Buddy slapped his cheek as the light bulb went on. "Jesus Christ, he's buying Anacott Steel."

The commander had readied his orders.

"Call François Devilier on his private line at Banque Privée de Zuriche. Tell him to park up to one million ANC shares in the bank's discretionary accounts, which he should pick up in foreign markets. To help *you* wet your wick a bit, use my credit to purchase up to 100,000 shares for yourself in a numbered Swiss account."

Buddy closed his eyes to help him fix the instructions in his memory, recalling Gordon's stern admonition never to write anything down. "Clean files," he had said.

"When the market opens tomorrow, buy two thousand September fifty calls. You getting all this?"

Bud nodded, then replied "yes" into the phone.

"Start buying blocks up to ten thousand shares, no bigger, a limit of fifty dollars per share. Ollie will go after the larger blocks. When Ollie gives the word, you can let out a little taste to your most trusted associates. Then call this number—555-7617; tell the man 'Blue Horseshoe loves Anacott Steel.' You *scored*, Bud. Be in touch." Click . . . Gekko was gone.

Gekko alerted Steeples. "Ollie, bid for large

blocks of ANC . . . ten thousand or more . . . and bid behind it. Paint the tape."

Buddy grabbed a cab to the Bluestar Airlines hangar, identified by a large company banner that hung from the rafters, BLUESTAR—THE VISION GOES ON. Beneath the exhortation, Carl Fox, Charlie Dent, and Dominick Amato were changing the generator on a 727. A welder repaired a wing seam. Bud shouted to his dad over the noise.

"Hey, Dad! Hi ya, Charlie . . . Dominick . . ."

Carl climbed off the maintenance stand and hugged his son. It felt good to Bud. He smiled, eager to share his good fortune.

"What brings you out here?"

"Client. Had a private jet over at Butler Aviation."

"How are things?"

"Great. New client, whole new league. It's starting to happen, Dad. The big league! You know what I'm saying." Bud pressed ten crisp $100 bills into his father's hand. "It's payback time, Dad."

"Sure, lots of guys at the track talk like that, but how do you know you'll have any dough next month?" Carl looked at the $1000. "Keep it, Buddy, I don't need it."

"Buy something wonderful for Mom. Send a cassette player and tapes to Bobby—not too much music on those aircraft carriers in the Persian Gulf. *Please* keep it."

Carl was touched by the renaissance in his son's spirit and decided to support it by taking the gift; but he was still uneasy with the quick turnaround.

"Problem with money is you never have enough or you got too much—and when you got it, you're never happy 'cause somebody's always trying to take it away from you. Money's one giant pain in the ass if you ask me. . . . thanks, Bud."

"Dad, how about dinner some night, with Mom too?"

"Whatever night you like."

"Wait . . . next week's booked. I'll check my calendar and get back to you."

Carl overlooked the pretentiousness of his son's reply. "Yeah, you do that, kid. I'll still be here."

Buddy was in orbit, and Carl Fox feared that gravity would punish such audacity.

CHAPTER XI

F_{ox} and Sidney Cohen, senior equity trader at Jackson & Steinhem, huddled briefly on the trading floor before withdrawing to a small glass-enclosed office behind the block desk. They diagnosed Anacott's market characteristics like surgeons studying a patient's medical history.

Sid punched "B-page . . . ANC . . . All Equity" into his computer. The screen displayed institutional holders of ANC in alphabetical order, accompanied by statistics on size as well as dates and approximate prices of purchases or sales in the stock. Internal data were supplemented with Spectrum, a quarterly edition of holdings by mutual funds, money managers, pensions, insurance companies, and bank trust departments. Graphs tracing volume and price action were analyzed. Finally, with the "harumph" of one about to make a weighty pronouncement, Sidney opined: "We can accumulate two million shares on the Exchange in about three months, given your fifty-dollar price limit and absolute secrecy. Alternatively, if your client *demands* it, we would solicit blocks directly from the institutions, while continuing to buy on the Exchange."

Bobby Smith, a block trader, stuck his head in and interrupted without apology: "200,000 Digital Equipment being offered at 162 . . ."

Cohen thought for half a second. "Take it and go short 200,000 IBMs until you can lay off the block."

Cohen returned to the Anacott deal. "You should know that in the old days, the firm refused to do direct solicitations of institutional clients in such situations. We had tight relationships with the customers on the sales side and didn't want to blindside them shortly before a higher bid came forth. However, loyalties have so eroded in the commission business that we are now willing to deal with the institutions at arm's length . . . so, if your client doesn't mind fouling his nest with the big boys, we'll solicit them, accumulate the block in four to six weeks at most."

Bud was uncharacteristically decisive. "Fuck 'em! Every animal has to learn to hunt for itself. My client owes nothing to the institutions. Burn 'em if you have to."

A code was assigned to the account. G-081's identity could be accessed only on a need-to-know basis. The meeting ended.

"Okay, Buddy . . . good work."

Bud respected the need for secrecy; he did not list ANC on his market minder or mention it to anyone. Periodically, he cocked a cautious eye at the tape, as it sped by with its intermittent update: 5000 ANC 45¾; 9000 ANC 46; 1000 ANC 45⅞; 6000 ANC 46⅝; 7500 ANC 46¼; 10,000 ANC 47⅛.

The deal came together on Thursday of the third week. Jackson & Steinhem had accumulated two million shares. Although Gekko would not tell Buddy of Ollie's activities, he did say Steeples was progressing with his usual finesse.

Buddy felt it was time to give his friends a small taste. He leaned over to Marv and whispered in his ear, "Anacott Steel . . . for your *best* customers."

Unhesitatingly, Marv hit a direct line to a large institution in Minneapolis. A prim, intense young lady in an Ann Taylor suit answered. She lowered the glasses on the bridge of her nose at the sound of Wycoff's voice.

"Laura, I injected a little cancer into your portfolio with that Hubbard Communications offering, but I'm gonna make it up to you. I've got real fancy information—buy Anacott Steel."

Buddy walked around to Hickey. He interrupted Dan's telephone conversation with an unexpected press on the hold button. Dan swiveled around, surprised to see such a determined, cold look on Buddy's face.

"Dan . . . Anacott Steel . . ."

Hickey nodded as he reactivated his telephone conversation. "Lasker, I just heard the loveliest two words—Anacott Steel . . ."

Chucky Cushing overheard the tip. "Hey, Buddy boy . . . think I should take a taste of Anacott? A light snack, of course."

"Yeah, why not."

"We ought to play tennis next week, at Rolling Rock."

"Thanks, Chucky. As soon as I can get out from under my workload."

"Right on, baby . . . you're really sharking your way up under the new regime."

Buddy was planning ahead when he approached Billy Glass. He sat down next to him.

"How ya doing, Billy?"

"Not too bad. Holding on."

"I've got some very special information—buy Anacott Steel, for your personal account."

"Are you sure, Buddy? I was counting on that partnership. I'm overextended, can't afford a loss."

"Buy it!"

"Thanks, Bud. Hope I can pay you back some day."

"Don't worry. If I need a small service, I'll call on you. Good luck!"

Several hours later, Lou Manheim wandered up to

Bud in his normal "walking and talking" mode. He sat down on Bud's desk, his mood somewhat more somber than usual.

"Heard one of the fellas recommending Anacott Steel. Not a very sound company anymore . . . but he was telling the customer it was a 'sure thing.' Ain't no such thing—'cept death and taxes. Do *you* know something?"

Both men seemed uncomfortable when Buddy assured him that there was nothing he could "disclose at this time."

"Remember, there are no short cuts, son. Quick-buck artists come and go with every bull market, but the steady players make it through all markets. You're part of something on Wall Street. The money we invest for people creates science, jobs, goods and services. And you, you're a young man . . . you've got a whole future ahead of you. Don't sell it all out."

Buddy was trapped in his seat, although all of his instincts screamed for flight. His apparent deference to Mr. Manheim was tinged by a subtle defiance.

"You're right, Mr. Manheim, but you gotta get to the big time first . . . then you can be a pillar and do good things."

Manheim rose from his perch, a pensive furrow in his brow.

"Can't be a little bit pregnant, Buddy. Be careful."

CHAPTER XII

An alarm cracked the dawn. Buddy sat upright in his bed and grimaced at the clock face showing 4:30 A.M. He fumbled for a crumpled slip of paper with a telephone number scribbled on it, then reached over to a small bedside table and pulled the telephone cord across the sheet. With a trembling hand he dialed 011-411-21-02-14. François Devilier picked up the private line on the corner of his rolltop desk in the ornate partners' room of Banque Priveé de Zuriche.

"Qui?"

At the easy, assured sound of François's voice, Buddy's apprehension disappeared.

"Hello."

"Bonjour." Devilier's thin lips barely parted; his

eyes darted around the perimeter to reaffirm his privacy.

"Did you buy 100,000 shares for my account?"

"Mais qui, monsieur."

"And the million shares for the bank's discretionary accounts?"

"Yes! Bud, what is the probability of a bid?"

"A fact!" Buddy exclaimed. "After our friend files a 13D with the SEC saying he owns eight percent of the company, you will sell the bank's shares to him at a three million profit. With the stock you parked for us, we already unofficially have a fifteen percent stake in Anacott Steel."

"Understood! Au revoir."

Buddy couldn't fall asleep. Sit-ups, push-ups, and jogging in place did little to relieve his tension. Bud audited the braking cars and occasional music on Columbus Avenue. He traced every shadow in the tiny bedroom a hundred times. At 7:30 A.M. Bud made another call.

"Newsroom. Farrell here." The graveyard shift was almost over at *The Financial Journal*. Farrell was drinking his last cup of coffee to make it through the assignment.

Buddy spoke into the receiver in a hushed voice.

"Blue Horseshoe loves Anacott Steel." He hung up.

The young reporter quickly thumbed through "arbitrageurs" on his Rolodex. Arbitrageurs—a breed who bet fortunes on companies they believed would soon be taken over at higher stock prices. After a raider acquired a cheap block of shares in a corporate target, he sometimes used the rumor mill to signal the arbs, like a howl to the pack, to take huge stock positions in anticipation of a quick killing on a takeover. A target was thus put *in play*. The surrounded victim was pressured to believe that it could not survive as an independent company. If the raider's tactics succeeded, management's sole focus would become how to sell the company while preserving its own jobs and perks.

Farrell called Howie Rudin.

"I'm trying to verify an anonymous tip. Probably nothing. Hear anything about Anacott Steel?"

Rudin punched up the last three months of stock volume on his Quotron. Green columns of numbers illuminated the black screen, showing overall a large daily volume of shares being transacted at gradually escalating prices.

"Charts show the shares are being accumulated."

"Thanks, Rudy."

Rudin glanced at his trader. "Buy 100,000 Anacott Steel. Something may be happening."

The trader hit a direct line to a third market dealer on the West Coast; wholesale blocks of stock were bought and sold here prior to the opening of the big board in New York.

"Charlie, 100,000 AST to buy . . . quarter over the close."

"I can offer 30,000 at the quarter, the balance at three-eighths."

"Done!"

Farrell called Ronnie Borgia, a knowledgeable curmudgeon at Dinkins, Berger and Borgia. "Borg, you hear anything in the arb community about Anacott Steel?"

"Rumor is that Wildman is sniffing around it. The merchandise is in the window...only a matter of time till someone picks it up. This firm already has a position."

"Thank you."

"Add 50,000 shares to Arbitrage Fund II's position in AST," he alerted his trader.

Meanwhile, Farrell rushed to his editor.

"Anacott Steel is in play! Our favorite anonymous tipster, Blue Horseshoe, called. I confirmed with two arbs that something may be up."

"Run a story for tomorrow's edition; handle it strictly as a rumor."

Buddy made his final call. "Good morning, Mr. Gekko. You control fifteen percent of Anacott Steel. Blue Horseshoe put the stock in play, per your instructions."

"Great work, Buddy boy. I knew you had the right stuff."

"Thank you, sir."

Buddy crumpled into his green-velvet easy chair. He felt so pleasantly exhausted and relaxed. It was better than sex. Bud Fox would no longer be an

anonymous cog in the financial machine of Jackson
& Steinhem. He was a player now—and soon to be a
rich one. Gekko and Fox were partners!

$ $ $

Buddy felt confident in his future. He kept to his
daily routine of slipping into a blue sweatsuit and
jogging around Central Park Reservoir. His face reflected youthful hope—full cheeks, smooth, pale skin
accented by dark, wavy hair, lips relaxed into a thin
smile of satisfaction with the status quo. Buddy's six-
foot muscular frame bobbed up and down in the flat
light, observed by an army of the homeless lying on the
benches surrounding the track. Only Buddy's steel-
gray eyes betrayed a deep loneliness, peering outward
in a desperate desire to please others, something his
witnesses on the benches no longer needed to do.

$ $ $

Gekko flipped on the CNN Business Report in his
East Hampton summer home. Anacott Steel was the
lead story.

"...the big story this afternoon is Anacott Steel,
trading at fifty-one and an eighth on heavy volume.
A rumored takeover attempt was reported on the
News Service. In response to an inquiry from the
New York Stock Exchange, management issued a
terse 'no comment.' Sir Laurence Wildman, specu-
lated to be a possible acquirer, did not return phone
calls. Analysts believe the company may be worth

seventy-five dollars per share in a hostile bid."

A Chinese houseboy entered Mr. Gekko's library. "Calls for you, sir. A reporter from the *New York Times* on two . . . says it's important . . . and a Mister Fox on three . . . says it's urgent."

"I came to the country, and it's worse than in the city! Tell the reporter I'll call back." He answered Buddy's call, "Yeah."

Buddy was speeding along on the high of unfolding events.

"We control 3.1 million shares and 2000 November 50 options' contracts. Average unit cost of $48 . . . $4 per share for the call. I just wish we bought more."

"Don't expect it all, sport, or you'll burn out. First rule of business is never get emotional about stock . . . clouds the judgment. Where do we stand?"

"We've invested $149.6 million. At this point we're up $7.3 million—net. If ANC goes at the analysts' estimates of $75 per share, we stand to net a cool $80.6 million . . . including $2.28 million on my 100,000 share position."

Gekko felt the anticipation of a hunter watching from the bush as his prey reached for the bait that would spring his trap.

"I expect Sir Larry is choking on his royal chamber pot by now."

Bud inserted an apologetic bureaucratic tone into the conversation. "Sir, the firm needs your signature on these options agreements by tonight."

"Can't it wait? I'm good for it."

"But, sir . . . it's a legal requirement."

"Awright. Come out to East Hampton. Get the directions from Natalie."

CHAPTER XIII

Gekko had crushed his natural feelings in the single-minded pursuit of greed. Growing self-awareness made him more insecure and bitter, justifying greater ruthlessness in seeking financial compensation for his sacrifice.

Gordon joined his wife, Kate, on the broad gray porch that swept around their Victorian home. Kate loved the East Hampton home in which she had spent every summer since her birth, as had her mother, grandmother, and great-grandmother. When her father's will divided his fortune among the children, she appreciated his respect and affection for her in specifying Kate as mistress of this house.

The carved gingerbread posts framed the natural portraiture before the house. Deserted sand dunes absorbed the sunset, radiating a golden yellow glow, as if a soul had penetrated the loneliness. Everything was still and peaceful, yet nothing was stagnant. The land sloped from the house into reeds and cattails that shimmered their reflections in a quiet pond that licked the dunes, dunes pressed against dark sea and pale sky on the horizon. The elements blended and transformed endlessly in the evening light, while the crash and recession of the waves etched a sense of the eternal on the landscape.

Gekko paced restlessly along the porch, awaiting Wildman's next move. He observed how the house commanded the land, organically growing out of the earth in layers, like a giant elm tree, porch, living rooms, bedrooms, attic, and widow's walk rising gently, like the swell in the ocean facing it.

"Kate, I hate this house. It mocks me . . . gives the illusion that you can hold things still . . . when nothing is permanent."

Gordon could not understand the irony in his comment. When Kate had told her father she was going to marry Gordon, he had objected strongly. What Kate saw as a self-made millionaire, her father regarded as a parvenu. When she said Gordon was strong and refreshing compared with the wilting personalities of the young men she grew up with, he replied, "But will your real-estate man appreciate this house . . . think, Kate."

Kate was concerned with Gordon's increasing hollowness, and enveloping joylessness.

110

"Gordon, give up this constant combat. You never stop working long enough to have a good time. You never see me or your son. What's the money for, if we can't enjoy it?"

Gekko was maudlin. He paced the length of the porch.

"Work means everything to me, Kate. I can never settle down."

Kate was depressed and frustrated. She instinctively reached for a club. "Let go . . . mellow out . . . you're not a poor kid from Campsville anymore."

Gordon plucked a geranium from Kate's white flowerbox on the porch and ripped its petals off, one by one.

A giant shadow crossed the green lawn, as hundreds of wild Canadian geese passed overhead in V-formations on the migration flyway.

"Oh, Gordon . . . look at the geese."

Gordon craned his neck toward the sky. Resignation hung over him.

"Kate, I wish I could be free . . . but it's not *my* nature."

He took Kate's hand and pointed to their perfectly bred Norwich terrier, chewing something far away in the fields. His exquisite grooming added to the aura of Jackson's timelessness; he would have been a valued pet in any high civilization.

"We feed Jackson steak, veal, chicken—the best. Let him out into the fields, and the first thing he does

111

is kill a mouse . . . and loves it. It's his nature to kill and chew field mice . . . he's a dog."

It was time for Kate and Gordon to attend to imminent social duties. They walked to the end of the porch to greet their dinner guests. The driveway looked like a foreign auto show: Rolls Royce, Mercedes, Jaguar, Ferrari. The highlight was Steve Livingston's 1951 white Mercedes convertible, in mint condition. Odd among the polished hardware was a 1986 Buick, which belonged to Professor Morris Heller, Pulitzer Prize-winning novelist, and high on everybody's Hampton guest list.

The men wore standard-issue white, green, or red pleated cotton trousers, with matching polo shirts or pastel baggy sweaters. Sockless feet were protected by Italian loafers and docksiders. The ladies wore silk camisole tops and cotton or silk slacks, jumpsuits, and sundresses. Only their megacarat diamond rings and simple gold-link Bulgari chains with their antique coins indicated anything unusual about the status of these people.

The Gekkos did not have close friends, in the realm of sharing personal intimacies. Gordon selected all of the couple's friends primarily for entertainment value, rather than on the basis of loyalty, sensitivity, or knowledge. Much the same thing could be said about the others at his party.

A waiter on the porch offered the guests champagne or took their desired drink orders. The selections were simple: white wine, vodka, gin, and an occasional martini. Cocktails were served on a patio adjacent to the large, lighted pool, while sushi, caviar, gravlox, and cucumber hors d'oeuvres were presented to the guests. The cook roasted lamb and grilled tuna steaks at a corner of the pool. Two tables set for eight in the dining room would receive the diners. Each table had a small centerpiece of multicolored dahlias, picked from Kate's flower garden.

Conversations were easy, emphasizing places they'd recently been; stories about romances, affairs, and divorces; movies or books; and individual sports.

"Florence was terrific . . . I never tire of the Medici collections . . ."

"I couldn't imagine that Henry Ames was having an affair with the flower girl on Lexington Avenue . . . I guess Maggie couldn't either "

The Big Chill brought me right back to my college days . . . picketing the Pentagon . . ."

"Racing out of Dark Harbor was great this year . . . steady wind . . ."

Money and business were rarely mentioned, except in the context of exploding real-estate prices in the Hamptons.

Bud arrived from the city in his business suit. He announced himself to the butler.

"Bud Fox. I have some papers for Mr. Gekko to sign."

Without thinking, the butler closed the door and left Bud on the porch with a terse, "Please wait a moment."

He went through the house and informed Mrs. Gekko that Mr. Fox was here to get some papers signed. Kate recognized the name and walked around the porch to greet Buddy.

"Hello, I'm Kate Gekko. You came from the city?" Buddy nodded. "Long drive... leave your papers with the butler and join us for a drink."

As Buddy approached, Gordon looked at his clothes.

"If you'd rather I not stay, Mr. Gekko, I can leave..." A tone of hope punctuated Buddy's disclaimer.

"Yeah, why not stay, Buddy boy. Get rid of the tie and jacket, roll up your sleeves... join the party. I'll introduce you around."

Bud suppressed a gasp and strained to remain expressionless when Gordon introduced him to Darien Taylor, the beautiful blonde whose disappearance he had been lamenting for weeks. Darien did not recognize him. She was still with Mr. GQ, now graced with the name of Steve Livingston. Buddy moved on through the crowd beside Gordon, his heart beating wildly.

Following the introductions, Bud spent most of his time observing and listening to the conversations of others. These people were not terribly interested in the opinions or experiences of outsiders. All the while, he kept a cautious eye on Darien, as on the stock tape in his office, waiting for the moment when she would break away from the group. He was determined never to lose her again.

The Chinese houseboy whispered in Gordon's ear. Gekko tensed but unhurriedly picked up a cellular phone lying on a table at poolside.

"Larry, what a surprise . . . Can it wait till tomorrow? I got some people over . . . If you feel that way, Larry, come over."

$ $ $

Wildman ordered the captain to reverse the direction of his yacht and head for the Montauk Yacht Club.

"Tell the driver to pick up my lawyer, Arthur Milcus, in Bridgehampton and meet me with him in tow at the Club. We'll leave for East Hampton immediately upon landing."

Sir Laurence Wildman turned on his radio-operated computer and activated a program on Anacott Steel. His expression became gnarled in anger as he kicked a life preserver overboard.

"That pissant. I'll cut his heart out."

$ $ $

Darien quit the poolside and walked into the living room to examine a sculpture. Bud seized the moment and followed her. He approached Darien with two glasses of calvados in hand.

"Hello again, I've been holding these drinks for us for the last three weeks."

115

"Excuse me?"

"Grand Marnier."

"Oh, yes, I remember you."

Bud felt encouraged when Darien reached for her drink.

"Destiny took us apart, but I knew it would bring us back together."

"Aha. Poet or philosopher?"

"Gordon's stockbroker. As in, never have so few done so little for so much."

Buddy anxiously tested what type of conversation might engage Darien's continued interest. He focused on a painting of a buffalo skull in the desert, which hung on the wall in front of them.

"What do you think Gordon sees in such a painting?"

"I'd give anything to have this in my house, even for a week."

"I hope not more than a few grand."

"Oh, really? Well, I guess you can kiss your career as an art appraiser goodbye, because *we* paid over four hundred thousand dollars for it at the contemporary picture sale last June. It's a Georgia O'Keeffe."

When Darien said "we," Bud's memory was rocked back to the scene outside of Nell's. He had thought that he had seen Darien before. She was the gorgeous blonde hanging onto Gekko's hand as they brushed past the crowd on the sidewalk outside Nell's. Now that he knew she had a relationship with

Gekko, he desired her even more . . . if that was possible. Darien was the ultimate prize!

"I gather you're a decorator."

"You got it—a great spender of other people's money."

"Well, if you're that good, you could probably do wonders at my place."

"Where is it?"

"Upper West Side."

Darien's interest faded rapidly. Buddy groped for a prop. "Oh, it's just a rental. I'm moving to the East Side soon. I've got a couple of deals brewing with Gordon. . . . How about having dinner with me on Friday? The Quilted Giraffe."

"What if I have a previous engagement?"

"Break it."

Darien calculated her reply for a moment. She sighed an almost inaudible, "oh well," and shrugged her shoulders.

"I guess this must be destiny all right. My first yuppie apartment and"—she patted him on the cheek flirtatiously—"my first yuppie."

"You may call me a yuppie . . . it's *Mister* Yuppie to you."

They both laughed.

"So, see you Friday."

"You really do believe in destiny?"

"Only if I want something bad enough."

Steve Livingston and Kate entered the living room. "There you go again, Darien, talking with strange men. I can't bring you anywhere."

"That's our Darien . . . Mr. Livingston . . . elusive, reclusive, exclusive. You know Buddy, right? He works for Gordon. . . . You staying for dinner, Bud?"

Buddy hesitated, his eyes on Darien. Kate shifted her attention as the doorbell rang.

"Excuse me for a second."

Steve Livingston whispered some amusing intimacy in Darien's ear. They both laughed and glided off. She looked over her shoulder at Buddy with a smile.

"Call me next week. I'll give you an estimate."

Buddy landed on Venus. Nevertheless he was a bit uneasy at having been so pretentious with Darien. But it had worked. The experience confirmed what Buddy was thinking all along. Power and money were the best aphrodisiacs!

CHAPTER XIV

Sir Laurence Wildman entered the foyer. His dark blue blazer hung perfectly over a white-knit cotton shirt and pressed white cotton trousers. A family crest of a united Bible and sword, purchased from faltering British nobility, emblazoned his breast pocket. Sir Laurence was a man of endless disguises; however, the heraldic emblem failed to soften his rapacious eaglelike face, aggressively on attack. Kate had to rely on all of her unbringing to manage a restrained greeting.

"Larry, how have you been? Get you a drink?"

His impatience was difficult to conceal, with Gordon not in sight.

"Oh, fine . . . nothing, thank you. Is—"

"Gordon? He'll be right here."

Gekko sauntered casually forward, chewing some food, with a napkin and drink in his hand.

"Larry! Excuse me, *Sir* Larry." Gordon's eyes were fixed on the crest. "Great to see you again. You're looking good."

Sir Laurence sniffed the air, glanced at the expensive modern art hanging on the Victorian walls, and turned to Kate with feigned nostalgia.

"Your father was an extraordinary man. I always *remember* this as a great American house."

Buddy was ill at ease. As Kate politely excused herself to rejoin her guests, Bud saw an opportunity for withdrawal.

"I guess I'll head back, Mr. Gekko."

Gordon viewed Arthur Milcus as Sir Larry's second in the forthcoming duel. He wished to maintain symmetry. It would also be so much more fun to skin Wildman at a public execution.

"Stick around . . . Larry, one of my gang—Bud Fox."

Wildman didn't acknowledge Fox's hello.

"Can we get down to business . . . Gordon."

"It's such a pleasant evening, why don't we sit on the porch."

The orange autumn moon hung between the posts at the end of the porch. As the four men sat hunched in the oversized wicker chairs, their profiles resembled black one-dimensional cutouts in the moonlight.

"What is your sudden interest in Anacott Steel?"

"The same as yours, Larry. Money. I thought it

would be a good investment for my kid."

"No. This time it's more than money. I'm in it to rebuild the company. This is *not* a liquidation, Gordon. You're getting a free ride on my tail, mate, and with the dollars you're costing me to buy in the stock, I could modernize the plants." He mustered his long suppressed cockney accent to show his sympathy for the working class. "I'm not the only one who pays here, Gordon. We're talking about lives and jobs, three and four generations of steel workers . . ."

Each man stared, soullessly, straight into the eyes of the other. Men of no dreams—entertaining nothing but the immediate and practical.

"You must be wearing a mask, you're laughing so deliriously behind it, Larry. Let's cut the 'sir' crap. Correct me if I'm wrong. Once you had the management safely in your pocket and took over CNX Electronics, you laid off eight thousand workers; Jackson Fruit, about six thousand; that airline . . ."

"Don't give me history lessons, Gekko. I came from a steel workers' family. I want to restore this company . . . as a matter of principle."

Gekko responded witheringly. "Let us not over-dignify ourselves. We're not men of principle—despite that Bible and sword you wear on your tailored blazer. We survive by short-term responses to need and greed!"

He paused. "What do you really want, Wildman? How much? And when?"

Wildman's pretense evaporated; his voice was cold

and controlled. "I could break you, mate, in two pieces, over my knees—you know it . . . I know it. I could dump the stock just to burn your bottom, but I happen to want the company and I want your block of shares. I'm announcing a tender offer at sixty-five tomorrow, and I'm expecting your commitment."

Buddy waited for the shootout. Gekko remained calm; he controlled the playing field . . . so long as he didn't go too far.

"Please . . . no threats. I hate showdowns. Everyone loses when emotions unleash uncontrollable forces. You can defeat me in an all-out war, but we both know your agenda at Anacott Steel can't be satisfied as long as I'm pissing in the soup. One of us has to step aside. I blinked last time; now it's your turn . . . Sir Laurence."

Gekko turned to Buddy. "What do you think is a fair price for *our* stock, Bud?"

All eyes shifted to Buddy. After a millisecond of panic, he focused on *his* own 100,000 shares of Anacott, in the Swiss numbered account. He was as cold and ruthless as his mentor.

"The breakup value is higher than sixty-five. It's worth eighty."

Gekko injected a feigned concern. "But we don't want to be greedy, now, so let's let him have it at seventy-two."

Wildman's eyes were icy-mean. "You're a pirate, Gekko. Not only would you sell your mother to make a deal, you'd send her COD . . ."

Gekko was ready to play his last card. He deliberately displayed his anger and rose to return to the party. Wildman stood up and coolly uttered one word.

"Seventy-one."

"Considering you brought my mother into it, seventy-one fifty."

"Done. You'll hear from my lawyers. Eight A.M." His goodnight intoned the certainty of a rematch with a different outcome on another playing field. He stalked away.

Gekko turned to Bud like a medical professor dissecting a case for an intern on rounds.

"He's right. I *had* to sell. The keys to this game are your capital reserves and credit. You don't have enough, you can't pee in the tall weeds with the big dogs."

Bud echoed his teacher, to show how well he had mastered the lessons. "All warfare is based on deception. Sun Tzu says if your enemy is superior, evade him; if angry, imitate him; if equally matched, fight . . . if not, split and reevaluate."

Gekko flashed a genuine smile of satisfaction— more relief at Wildman's capitulation than amusement with Buddy's act—as they returned to Kate's dinner party.

"You're learning, sport . . ."

Buddy had never seen Gordon so happy.

CHAPTER XV

The persistent ocean wind rolled up the window shade in Bud's guest room, framing Gordon as he stood alone on the fog-shrouded porch, exhaustion paling his face. A cellular telephone filled his right hand.

Gekko's figure was protected from the damp autumn chill by a yellow slicker over a blue boatneck sweater and high Timberland boots. Bud hurriedly pulled on his chinos, a thin Polo shirt, and Gucci loafers to join Gekko on the porch.

"Good morning, Gordon . . . what're you doing up so early?"

"Money never sleeps, pal. When I came in in 'sixty-nine, they traded six hours a day; now the clock don't stop, London's deregulated, the Orient is hungrier than us. Just let the money circle the world, sport, buying and selling, and if you're smart it comes back paying. I just made $800,000 in Hong Kong gold."

"I couldn't sleep, Gordon. I was so excited by what we did last night. My mind kept churning . . . what do we do next?"

Gordon reacted to the youth's eagerness.

"What's next, sport, is that you're going to get pneumonia. Go inside, borrow warm clothes and boots . . . the mist penetrates everything."

Bud returned in an outfit identical to the one that Gordon wore, and they walked over the dunes. The solitary figures were matted against the fog, like dark papers on a gray cardboard collage. The roofline disappeared in the thickness; trees and dunes were etched like particles that had lost their binding matter. A foghorn sounded so commandingly in the distance that one believed he actually saw the invisible tanker.

Gekko and Fox were totally oblivious to their surroundings, with endless talk about deals, junk bonds, liquidations—money, money, money. The restless gestures of these cerebral gymnasts moved in sharp angles, scalpels cutting open the fog's smooth skin. Gordon pointed down the beach.

"You want to know what to do next? Study that fisherman."

The old surfcaster was hardly noticeable in his black slicker and cape-cod hat. His small eyes were like coals staring straight out to sea. The angler's arms were bent at the elbow in a V shape; they moved with the swells as he adjusted his line to meet the changing conditions of the surf. Gordon watched admiringly: "Pursue opportunity . . . again and again."

Buddy was glad to see the conversation take a practical turn. "How do we identify the opportunity?"

"What do you see where the fisherman is casting his line?"

"Water . . . waves . . ."

Gordon had a disappointed look. "Seagulls, attacking the surf. He's casting into a run of bluefish. A smart fisherman watches other fishermen . . . he casts where they tell him to."

"Which stock group do we fish in, Gordon?"

Gekko hesitated to give weight to the point he was going to make, like a teacher about to summarize the lesson.

"Gulls are the wisest fishermen. Primarily, they are scavengers. No hunting . . . no uncertainty . . . no risk. If they must fish, they dive for ready prey: no speculation . . . no wasted motion—sure things, sport."

"So?"

"So get information. I don't care where or how, just *get* it . . . takeovers, mergers, restructurings—sure things! Find smart guys you can trust who want to share in the goodies.

"And here's some inside info for you. My wife tells me you made a move on Darien. Mister GQ has big bucks, but he's boring her to death. The exit visa is imminent . . . so don't lose your place in line. If you listen to me, I'm gonna make you rich enough so you can afford Darien."

Buddy loved it. He ruminated aloud: "Billy Glass could be perfect. Head of the junk bond department at Jackson & Steinhem . . . knows about every takeover in advance . . . got screwed by the firm . . . needs walking money. Bit of a loner, though."

"Loner is perfect. No supermen need apply . . . just steady fishermen."

"Then I have an old college roommate who's an M and A lawyer at Botts, Barnes and Dorrance. Went to law school to please his father, who's a senior partner. Bored to death and always cursing his investment-banker classmates who're making three times his income. . . . Then there's David Fine . . ."

Gekko listened approvingly. "Okay, school is out now. You know how the game is played; go to work on it. There's an old Russian proverb, 'A fisherman always sees another fisherman from afar.'"

Gordon puzzled over whether Buddy's boyish indifference to danger was a sign of courage or a childlike expectation that, somehow, someone or something would take care of him when things went wrong.

"At noon I would like you to join me for lunch

with Harold Solomon, my personal lawyer."

"Great! Love to."

$ $ $

Lunch was served on the red-brick patio overlooking the swimming pool. The houseboy provided a choice of tuna salad prepared with a light vinaigrette or cold lobster and mayonnaise. A California chardonnay rested in the silver ice bucket beside the small glass-topped wrought-iron table.

Harold Solomon had just flown into East Hampton Airport on Gordon's jet. Despite his best efforts, he still looked a bit uncomfortable in the country. Thick glasses sat on a rounded, protruding nose; they presided over smart eyes flanked by heavy bags of worry, which could only have come from watching over other people's money. Harold's double-breasted blue blazer, white shirt, and gray silk tie did little to loosen his image. Indeed, he looked as if he were used to spending his Saturdays at the office or in Madison Avenue art galleries, rather than at poolside.

Wine was served while Harold busied himself putting paperwork in order. He unsmilingly passed the first pile of documents to Buddy, who took them with a relaxed receptivity.

"You understand Mr. Gekko is constantly harassed with nuisance litigation and IRS audits. So it's in both our interests to put a safe distance between you and us. . . . This gives you limited power-of-attorney for Mr. Gekko's account. Every trade you make is at your discretion. Every ticket you write must be marked 'solicited.' That means you call the shots, and Mr. Gekko has no official knowledge of what stocks you're buying. . . . Sign here and here . . ."

Gekko countersigned.

Now that the die was cast, Buddy glanced sideways at Gekko in a mute solicitation of reassurance; Gordon's casual smile fortified him.

"Just the beginning, sport, just the beginning . . ."

While Buddy signed unread document after document, Harold emphasized the underlying motif in a mildly concerned tone. "You understand if any problems arise, you're out there on your own. The trail stops with you."

Buddy zoomed through the caution light, buoyant on his new authority. He enthusiastically continued to sign originals, copies, endorsements, specimens with a show of bravado.

"That's cool, Harold, all's fair in love and war . . ."

To which Gekko interrupted, "The art of which is deception. Spread the buy orders through different accounts, and you won't get burned."

Harold added, "Mr. Gekko is particularly interested in Teldar Paper. We need more votes for the showdown, but we don't want to go public with an amendment of our SEC filing. You've got to park this stock with third parties."

Bud recalled the conversation on the beach. "I

think I have friends who won't mind sharing the wealth."

Harold told Bud to pay attention. "This is a contact at one of our banks. On settlement day you'll open an account there for Mr. Gekko under the name of Geneva, Roth Holding Corporation. Then you'll wire-transfer the money to this account in the Cayman Islands."

Gekko motioned to the houseboy that lunch was over as he left the table.

"Think about incorporating yourself there, Bud. Harold will take care of it for you, at a reasonable fee. You're gonna make a lot of money now, Bud . . . stakes are gonna go up, no mistakes . . ."

Bud mechanically shook hands with Harold. He smiled confidently at his mentor. "Piece of cake, Gordon."

Gekko had distanced himself from the legal consequences of his protégé's actions. Discretionary accounts gave him plausible "deniability" of knowledge, while enabling him to benefit from Bud's deeds.

$ $ $

Darien invited Bud to join her for a swim at the beach. The young couple bounded over the dunes and splashed directly into the waves; they dove into the breakers and bodysurfed their crests to shore for more than half an hour. Pleasantly exhausted, Darien and Bud emerged from the sea. His gaze was fixed on the sunlight reflecting off the water onto her lean, athletic body. Bud held forth a towel to wrap her splendor; she thanked him with a seductively inscrutable smile. Darien suddenly spun her body around 360 degrees, arms spread-eagled above her head, cool blue eyes devouring everything before them.

"If I could have anything, this would almost do."

"Yeah, almost . . ." He stifled his temptation to go further.

"So how did your conference go with Gordon and Harold?"

Bud was taken off-guard. "The conference, oh, yeah. Fine. We reached an agreement and decided to divide up the world between us."

Darien laughed. "You have modest wants. I like that in a man."

"And what do you want?"

Darien didn't have to think. "A Turner, a perfect canary diamond, a Lear jet . . . world peace . . . the best of everything . . ."

Bud responded playfully. "Well, why stop at that?"

A deadpan Darien retorted, "I don't."

Bud smiled. "You're not trouble by any chance, are you?"

Darien looked at him with an I'm-worth-it grin, tossed the towel over her shoulder, and ran back toward the house, with Buddy in hot pursuit.

CHAPTER XVI

On Tuesday, Bud planned a surprise visit to his former college roommate, Roger Barnes, at the law offices of Botts, Barnes & Dorrance. He walked briskly across a broad plaza filled with office workers heading home and entered 1223 Avenue of the Americas.

Since the bomb scare last year, no visitor could enter an elevator unannounced. Bud's surprise was blown when the security guard called Barnes for verification. As the elevator rocketed to the forty-third-floor reception area, Buddy determined from the tenant roster that Botts, Barnes & Dorrance occupied sixteen floors.

The neatly dressed receptionist leafed through a firm directory the size of a paperback novel to locate

Roger Barnes. "Baculey . . . Baldwin . . . Banner . . . Barnes, Roger . . . he's on fifty-six." She rang for a page. "Please escort Mr. Fox to room fifty-six-oh-four, juncture of corridors four and E. Thank you."

The firm's name and legacy was embossed in gold English script on the wall behind the reception desk: "Botts, Barnes & Dorrance, Esquires. Founded 1868."

The firm had been organized by three Yale classmates. By the close of World War II, it had forty-two attorneys, making it one of the large, establishment Wall Street firms. Its clientele included a money-center bank, a securities underwriter, and a multinational oil giant. In 1975 the firm had 150 lawyers crammed into its twisting corridors and wood-paneled offices at Two Wall Street. Law students referred to it as a factory, although they struggled desperately to be hired there. A decade later, Botts, Barnes & Dorrance had 435 lawyers and 2012 nonprofessional staff, was lodged uptown in a Sixth Avenue skyscraper, and boasted branches in London, Tokyo, Hong Kong, and Bahrain.

Senior lawyers nominally ran the firm through a five-member management committee; however, day-to-day authority had been delegated to a nonlawyer hierarchy—Administrator, Deputy Administrator, Office Manager, Deputy Office Manager, and so forth. An informal quota required that all professionals bill at least sixty hours per week. The overhead and pressures were so intense that those in charge winked at a discreet amount of padding clients' billable hours.

The offices were cells in a beehive, assigned according to rank: space, furnishings, decor, and equipment. Personal decorations were restricted to family desk photos. Botts, Barnes & Dorrance fostered a chilling anonymity, which produced specialists without spirit.

The page led Bud into room 5604. Roger Barnes communicated a cocky air as he stood to greet Buddy from behind his Knoll metal desk. He motioned familiarly to Bud to take a seat.

"Fox, Buddy D. You're not hitting me up for Dartmouth, are you?"

Buddy grinned. "Well, we're thinking of putting up a statue of you in the subway. I hear you're moving up in the world. A senior associate already . . . an expert in section 351 corporate mergers . . . not bad. How's Margie?"

Boredom and resignation permeated his tone. "Can't complain. She loves *her* house in Oyster Bay. Market treating you good? Still seeing that sexy French gal?"

Bud leaned forward in bemused intimacy. "Nah, she asked the wrong question."

"What was that?"

"'What are you thinking?' . . . that was it."

Roger chuckled, with a so-nothing's-changed shrug, as Bud continued.

"The hours are hell, but the money is starting to

tumble in. I know this guy who's got an ironclad way to make money. I can't lose, and I can't get hurt."

Roger straightened in his chair, all ears. "Does this guy have a tip for an honest lawyer?"

"Yeah, check out Teldar Paper, it's still not over." Roger nodded okay. "What about you, I hear you guys are handling the Fairchild Foods merger and it may not be going through. Any surprises I haven't read about in *The Wall Street Journal?*"

Roger rocked back in his chair.

"Come on, Bud, you wouldn't want to get me disbarred now, would you? Dad would have a heart attack."

Buddy mockingly surveyed the walls. "Who's listening? It's just one college roommate talking to another."

Roger tightened—the going was getting heavy; they were now in new territory.

"Relax, Roger, everybody's doing it."

Roger's brow wrinkled as he focused. He cupped his chin in his hands. "If I come aboard, what's in it for moi?"

Bud realized that Roger had toyed with the notion of insider trading before.

"More money than you ever *dreamed*, Roger. And the thing is, no one gets hurt. . . . How 'bout a beer?"

They had suddenly entered the negotiating phase. Buddy tried to remain nonchalant. Roger shook his head, as if to fortify himself.

"Too much to do . . . but I'll walk you out."

The firm's long, sparsely appointed hallways had the antiseptic look of hospital corridors, especially as the middle-aged female cleaning crews, in their faded green uniforms, moved in to perform their evening chores. A small, brown-skinned woman pulled a heavy commercial vacuum cleaner into a senior partner's office. It was obvious that Roger was still thinking about Bud's proposition when he said teasingly, "Get inside my father's door, Buddy, and all the secrets of the world are yours . . . the lifeblood of companies . . . the merger calendar . . . but you gotta go to law school first—or have the access code to his desktop computer, so you can identify the classified matters in the file room."

Buddy laughed and responded, only half-jokingly, "Give me an incentive to get through the magic door . . . to treasure hunt."

"V-seven-six-one."

Roger and Bud shook hands at the elevator. He entered the car and watched the metal doors squeeze shut. Fox exited the glass tower and walked casually around the corner to the loading dock. With a look of satisfaction normally reserved for picking the right stock, Bud sighted his prey: a van marked Marsala Maintenance Company. He jotted down the address in his pocket calendar and proceeded along the sidewalk with a mischievous look in his eyes.

$ $ $

Two days later Bud took a limousine over the Fifty-ninth Street Bridge, past the Silvercup neon sign, to Long Island City. The cobblestone streets were devoid of pedestrians in this commercial district of small factories and warehouses; burly teamsters loaded everything from Pepsi-Cola to Eagle Electric fixtures into long interstate trailers. The limo stopped at 121st Street and Jackson Avenue, before a shabby warehouse posted MARSALA MAINTENANCE AND GUARD SERVICE. An elderly chain-smoking lady received Bud in the bare reception room.

"I need to speak to Mr. Panos about business."

She glanced over his shoulder, through the barred window, to the idling limousine. "Please wait here."

Several minutes later, the woman reappeared and ushered Bud into the back office, with a slight bow and sweep of the hand. A middle-aged Greek with a bushy mustache and hardened face sat at a scarred wooden desk eating a fried-egg sandwich on a seeded roll, a large plastic container of coffee nested at his right elbow. The Greek had been working all night supervising the cleaning crews; he examined Bud through reddened, suspicious eyes. Fox handed him a card.

"Look, Mr. Fox, I don't buy no stocks. I prefer Atlantic City."

"Mr. Panos, I'm not here to sell you anything. I've charted the growth of new office space in the city, and I think you're in the right business at the right time."

Panos took a long sip of his coffee. "Thank you for telling me what I already know."

Buddy leaned in and lowered his voice to signal that he was getting serious. "I'm impressed with your work. I could also use a tax break by rapidly depreciating Marsala's equipment. Yours is a growing business. Are you interested in some working capital and . . . a partner?"

Panos kept his eyes riveted on Bud; he took a bite of his sandwich and measured the strange visitor. He replied carefully. "What makes you think I need a partner?"

Bud smiled, withdrew a bank cashier's check from his breast pocket, and handed it to Panos, with a look saying, "It's yours if you want it."

Panos gulped at the $1,000,000 stenciled onto the check, stood up, never letting go of the check, and shook Buddy's hand.

"Hello . . . partner!"

$ $ $

Panos was impressed that his new partner was not just a passive investor. Fox went into the field several times a week to inspect the cleaning crews.

The sound of clinking keys, on a heavy master key ring, preceded the passenger out of the elevator at Botts, Barnes & Dorrance. Fox emerged in a neatly pressed janitorial uniform, with MARSALA MAINTE-

NANCE emblazoned on the shirt pocket. He stopped to record the floor and time of his inspection: fifty-six at 8:10 P.M. Marsala's supervisor on duty introduced him as the boss to the cleaning crew and security guards. The cleaning women smiled politely and hurried off to do their chores, worried that any lesser show of diligence might cost them their jobs.

Fox strolled from office to office looking very official, overseeing the crew, and making notations on a clipboard. He used his master key to enter the senior partner's office. A brief inspection of the diary on his desk indicated the meetings that he had recently had with chief executives of companies rumored to be predators or takeover targets. Fox punched in the access code to the desktop computer—V761—which activated it. He input the names of the companies that he had isolated from the calendar and retrieved their coded file identification numbers.

Bud winked to the security guard as he entered the file room. His eyes busily scanned the territory as he spoke to the cleaning lady. "Annie, you did a fine job in here."

"Thank you, sir."

He glanced at his watch. "You better move on to the next area, if you're going to stay on schedule."

"Yes, sir. Have a good evening."

The active files were stored in neat manila envelopes on rows of steel shelves. Each file was identified only by a code number, specific for a particular client matter. Bud's eyes nervously examined the files. He found a file number that matched the client matter he had brought up on the computer screen in the partner's office. He untied the folder and inspected its contents. His eyes lit up when he found the key to the kingdom — a thick tender-offer document marked "DRAFT." The critical words were the target company's name: Rorker Electronics Corporation.

Fox carefully replaced the file and left Botts, Barnes & Dorrance with hearty compliments to his Marsala employees.

Buddy accumulated $5 million of Rorker Electronics stock in Gekko's nominee account in the Cayman Islands, Geneva, Roth Holding Corporation. He purchased an additional $1.5 million in his own Swiss numbered account. Fox was careful not to neglect Billy Glass, who was eager to invest on Bud's advice after the killing he had made on Anacott and other "special situations."

Bud continued to plug away at Jackson & Steinhem by day, while intercepting vital information at law firms and brokerage houses by night. The around-the-clock effort strung Bud out with exhaustion, but he was committed to building on his recent achievements; indeed, he became bolder with each score.

$ $ $

When Bud walked onto the trading floor Friday morning, he noticed immediately the uneasy silence that pervaded the room. Brokers milled around their cubicles, casting furtive looks in the direction of Hy Lynch's glass-enclosed office. A very somber Dan Hickey stood bowed before Lynch at his desk, like a defendant pleading to an indifferent judge who'd heard it all before. Bud turned to Marv in an effort to confirm his own sad assessment.

"What's going on?"

Marv flipped his head in the direction of the action. "Lynch is giving Dan the boot . . . he's not pulling the quota."

Dan's begging was intermittently heard through the glass.

"Hy, I helped build this firm . . . brought *you* in . . . I need the money . . . my kids are in college . . . I can't get another job at my age . . . you're destroying me . . . for Christ's sake give me a chance . . . we've been friends for thirty years. . . ."

Lynch was expressionless.

"No chances . . . I have my own problems . . . pressures . . . quotas are objective . . . nothing personal . . . I have no say over the outcome . . . you're out, Dan . . . don't make it harder on everyone."

As Lynch shook his head to illustrate his "no chances," Marv gave a quiet shudder and reminded himself as well as Buddy, "We're all just one trade away from humility."

Hickey stepped out of Lynch's office close to tears, trying to maintain whatever dignity was left to him. Dan walked by Buddy, a traumatized automaton. Fox cravenly averted his eyes. As Dan continued his painful walk down the narrow aisles of the trading floor, Lynch got on the microphone in his most matter-of-fact voice.

"New research report on GM and a conference call on defense stocks at my office at seven A.M. tomorrow. No RSVP required, just be there. And on an inspiring note, I'm pleased to announce that the new office record for a single month's gross commission from the rich man's business goes to Bud Fox. *Shows cold calling does work, fellows.* Way to go, Bud. Super job! Come on up here."

Bud rose from his seat; his eyes met the stricken man's across the cubicle. Dan tried to be brave, but both men were helpless. Meanwhile, attention in the room turned from Hickey to Fox, as the young salesmen and their assistants looked at him in awe and envy. Senior brokers' feelings of vulnerability increased. Marv patted Bud on the back and mumbled, "Congrats, Buddy, buddy, you just made my life twice as hard around here . . ."

Bud moved toward Lynch's office past Lou Manheim.

"You're on a roll, kiddo. Enjoy it while it lasts."

Bud recovered his bravado. "Just kickin' ass and taking names, Mr. Manheim. If you feel good, the customer feels good."

Fox knew he was riding high when Chuck Cushing ran up to him in the aisle. "When are we doing tennis at Rolling Rock? I want you to meet the membership."

"Any day now, Chucky..."

Lynch waved him into a small office, three down from his own.

"Congratulations. This is yours now. Your own file cabinets...a window...your private secretary, Janet. You can focus on running the big-ticket individual accounts unit."

Bud shook hands with Janet.

"Nice to meet you, Mr. Fox."

Bud was thrilled to be called *Mr.* Fox, thrilled to have an office and a secretary, thrilled to see his name plate on the desk.

"Thank you, Janet...uh, thank you, Mr. Lynch."

Lynch leaned on his bull's-head cane and affected his most unctuous smile.

"No... *thank you.* I knew the minute I laid eyes on you, you had what it takes, Bud. Just keep it going."

Lynch winked and left. Marv stuck his head in the doorway with a grudging smile. "So it's *Mister* Fox now."

$ $ $

Bill Glass was an important potential link in Fox's network, since he could provide advance information on takeover deals that required junk bond financing. Fox had deliberately gotten close to Glass. They both enjoyed lamenting their fates as victims of the process of conglomeration on Wall Street. Hickey's dismissal provided the perfect backdrop of fear for an approach to Glass. Buddy had already hooked Glass on profits garnered through the round-robin network of inside information from Gekko, Barnes, and Bud's own late-night intrusions. Buddy decided to approach the question at lunch.

"Ya know, after they screwed us at Jackson and Steinhem, I wisened up . . . learned to look out for number one."

"I know what you mean. The sale cheated me out of eleven years of work and millions of dollars. I still can't face my wife and explain why I stay here . . . except I need the big bucks . . . golden handcuffs."

Bud adopted the locker-room tone of team spirit. "Secure for how long? Look what they did to poor Hickey after thirty years. Ya know . . . we've done pretty well together in the stock market—so far. It will get bigger and better . . . enough to give you walking money and a lifetime of ease. But I need your help . . ."

"Talk to me, friend."

Earnestly and with a show of deep sympathy, Buddy continued, "You see, the parties who have been giving me the information want something in return—sure things . . . like they gave to us. You have the quid pro quo."

"Bud . . . that's illegal . . . unfair to the shareholders who sell to us without the same information. We'll lose our jobs . . . go to jail."

"Come on, who really gets hurt? It's ridiculous to have laws that regulate the free market, while muggers waste old ladies in the street. Jackson and Steinhem is our jail right now! We can buy our freedom. There is a justice, higher than the law."

Glass's greed welled up out of fear that the profits he was reaping from Buddy's sources would dry up.

"What do you have in mind, exactly?"

Bud set the hook. "You just give me an occasional tip . . . well in advance . . . sure things only. I pass it on to my friends, who buy the stock in offshore accounts . . . impossible for the SEC to detect or inspect. They win . . . cash goes into a numbered account in Switzerland . . . your percentage . . . and you get sure-shot investment tips from them, as well."

Billy's eyes and shoulders drooped with fatigue. "I guess after eleven years in the boiler room . . . I earned my freedom."

$ $ $

Bud continued to execute Gekko's instructions to spread large stock purchases over numerous individuals to disguise the size and source of the buy, which reduced the likelihood of regulatory monitors being alerted to a trade.

Fox had already developed a network of small brokers and individual acquaintances who were willing to be beards, for a small percentage of the profits, of course. He hoped to add an old friend, Dixon Bates, who had dropped out to become a long-haired ski bum in Aspen, Colorado. Dixon answered the phone half-drunk and was surprised to hear Bud's voice.

"Buddy . . . how come you're calling at this hour? Must be 4 A.M. back east."

"Money never sleeps, pal. I just got finished with my broker in Hong Kong . . . soon it will be time for London and Frankfurt . . . but never mind all that. I have a plan that will make us both a lot of money, with no risk."

Dixon heard the two magic words, "us" and "money"; he listened intently.

"Dixon? . . . Are you there?"

"Yeah . . . go ahead."

"Dixon, it's your lucky day! I want to give you some stock, and you don't have to put up a penny. . . ."

Dixon was skeptical. "Sure, and I'm never gonna die either. Is this one of those chain-letter schemes, or do I have to buy a door-to-door cosmetics franchise in North Dakota?"

Bud was getting frustrated with Dixon's fuzzy-headedness.

"No! No, Dixon, my client and I want to buy large—very large—blocks of stock, and we need to spread the orders around . . . put some in your name to preserve our privacy. I'll park some money in your account, and if it hits, you get a good cut. I'm telling you, this is the easiest money you ever made and you don't have to put up a dime."

Dixon's reply was tentative. "All right, Bud . . . let's do it."

"Great, Dixon. It's real simple. Open an account with a local broker, Rockland and Shane. I'll wire money into it today. Buy 200,000 shares of Teldar Paper over the next five weeks at market . . . spread it out, about 6000 shares per day—no more. That's it for now."

"Sounds like real work, making a call every day. What do I get out of it?"

"That's simple, sport! Ten percent of the gross. On sale settlement day, you endorse a check to Geneva, Roth Holding Corporation, Cayman Islands Bank, Ltd. The company will send your cut back."

"Sounds *too* easy. Any wrinkles?"

"None. That's the bottom line . . . and nobody gets hurt."

Dixon was now grinning. "Well, I always said you knew how to go for the gold! Gee, now I can afford to get really plastered tonight. Keep that Big Apple humming, Buddy. Goodnight."

That morning Dixon struggled with his hangover and made it to the brokerage house before he hit the slopes. The brokers initially regarded him with skepticism as he clunked into Rockland & Shane in his ski boots, poles and skis slung over his shoulder. However, Dixon was warmly received after he introduced himself, since Bud had already wired substantial funds into his account. Dixon wasted no time on small talk while he signed countless documents and cards. He placed his order with the broker.

"200,000 Teldar Paper at the market."

The broker seemed troubled. "Are you sure, sir? That's a lot of stock. You'll drive the price to the moon."

"I'm certain—200,000 Teldar. So long . . . I gotta take a few ski runs before the tourists mess up all the powder. Stay cool, man."

The broker made a face, a look of "I did my duty . . . these crazy kids have too much money."

$ $ $

The specialist on the New York Stock Exchange floor was surprised to see a 200,000 share market order in Teldar. He turned to Rockland's floor broker.

"Better verify this TLD order, Freddy."

Rockland's floor broker confirmed its accuracy by calling upstairs and returned to the window. The specialist was cautious.

"Something other than the proxy fight going on at Teldar?"

"Nothing I know of, Johnny."

The specialist held the order slip between his fingers while he thought for a second.

"Sure a big order for this baby. I can't short 200,000 and fill you . . . too thinly traded. How about taking 75,000 TLD share up three points; I'll work the balance."

"Okay, I'll hang around the booth."

The specialist yelled to his clerk to start looking for Teldar stock on the Midwest and Boston Exchanges. A floor reporter punched the trade into a computer on the side of the booth. Instantaneously, the trade flicked across stocktickers around the world: 75,000 TLD 25. It was shortly followed by another print on the tape of 125,000 TLD 26.

Three young men sat before computer screens at the New York Stock Exchange Stock Watch Office. The computers were programmed to identify unusual transactions in every stock traded on the Exchange, based upon historic prices, volumes, and trading patterns. The Teldar block flashed on the screen, as the computer started to beep. A stock watch officer punched up additional data about TLD. He attentively watched the tape. A stream of medium-sized buy orders flowed in from Buddy's network, adding to the unusual activity in TLD stock, which was triggered by Dixon.

An official of the Exchange was notified. He routinely telephoned the chief financial officer of Teldar Corporation and informed him of the activity in his stock. The official inquired, "Are you aware of any special reason for the increased volume and price of TLD?"

There was a long pause. "Must have something to do with the Gekko proxy fight."

"Thank you, Ray. The Exchange will stay in touch."

The Securities Exchange Commission was notified of the circumstances involving Teldar. A federal investigator from the regional office arrived at the Stock Watch Office and took a seat at the computer bank.

"Please give me all the information you have on Teldar Paper . . . and see if you can get a line on who the buyers are."

CHAPTER XVII

Bud finally understood the distinction that Gordon had made repeatedly, between being rich and being a well-to-do Wall Street working stiff, when he searched for an Upper East Side coop apartment. Even a broom closet on Fifth and Park avenues cost upward of $2 million, and this was only an invitation to a monthly maintenance charge that started at $2500.

Sylvie Drimmer, a real-estate agent from Geffen & Ehrlichman, was a short intense woman; she acted as if she had a taxi meter running at all times. Her plastic smile was a mask, obvious to herself and to everyone who she encountered, over the steely hardness that a widowed real-estate agent needed to survive in New York City. With her large costume pearls, fur cape, and fur pocketbook, Sylvie cut a particularly sorry figure on this clear fall day.

She defined Bud's status by taking him first to a thirty-story apartment building on Eighty-fourth Street and Third Avenue.

"This is a condominium, not a coop. No fancy boards to pass on admission. You like, it's yours... cash and carry."

The large hallway was reminiscent of an ornate hotel lobby. Young adults walked in and out ignoring their surroundings. Not a child was in sight. Sylvie sold the child-free environment.

"Mostly singles and young marrieds, suburban empty-nesters who want a pied-à-terre in the city. No kids to bother you."

Sylvie accepted a key from one of two concierges who stood behind a tall desk with a switchboard and 376 tiny mail boxes behind them.

"Best concierges... get the takeout food up to the apartment before it gets cold."

The elevator was paneled with synthetic "wood," which was impervious to defacement, as well as resistant to the human eye. They exited the elevator into a long, dimly lit hallway decorated with green-vinyl wall covering. Three unsmiling young women brushed past them into the elevator.

"Mr. Fox, it's great here... total privacy. Everybody is busy... sticks to himself... you don't have to know your neighbor... no less anybody else."

They entered the 3075 square feet of space: living room, dining alcove, kitchen, two bedrooms, and a balcony that one could just stand on.

"You can see Central Park from this balcony—there . . . right between those buildings."

The apartment was constructed of wallboard and had an eight-foot ceiling. Not a single curve or bit of molding existed; everything ended in sharp, clean right angles.

Sylvie took the initiative immediately, by selling something other than the apartment. Her spiel was clearly standard.

"Everybody tells you they hate the Upper East Side and they wanna live on the West Side, but, honey, when it comes to resale time, believe me the East Side's the one that always moves. What do you get on the West Side?"

Now Sylvie was contemptuous.

"Madonna and Sean? . . . with Sly and Billy and Christie. I've shown every apartment on the Upper East Side. Everybody lives here . . . Mick, Gloria, and Barbara Wa-Wa. Even Klaus von Bulow buys his fresh fruit from the Korean on Madison Avenue. It's so expensive, and it's just like the ones on Eighth Avenue, but it's an attitude is all, you pay for attitude . . . I can get you a ten percent mortgage . . . so? I got a four o'clock and a five . . . one of them's an all-cash type, Monique something or other . . . I guarantee you this place is history tomorrow. . . ."

Buddy still said nothing. He stood on the balcony

with the city at his feet. As he looked west, Queens was behind him and Manhattan was before him . . . at his feet. Bud was lost in thought when Sylvie snapped her fingers to call him out of it.

"Honey? The meter's running. Anybody home?"

Bud didn't turn around. "All right. Offer nine-fifty . . . in cash."

Although Sylvie tried to play it cool, her expression conveyed surprise at his rapid and certain response.

"I think you gotta deal, honey . . . you sure you don't wanna see somethin' I got on Sutton Place? It's a million and a half, but . . ."

"Nah. This is it . . . home."

He surveyed the apartment, then the city below, proud of his acquisition.

$ $ $

Bud made calls to Darien and Gordon from a pay phone on Eighty-fourth Street.

He had seen Darien frequently since the time they had spent together in East Hampton. It was a great combination. Darien knew what to do. He was Darien's age, unmarried, and had the income to do and get the things she normally had to depend on older or married men for—clothes from Ferragamo and Ralph Lauren; small jewelry from Bulgari; dinners at Café Society, Marcello, and Le Bernardin; shows like

A Chorus Line, *Cats*, *Les Misérables*; dancing at the Surf Club and Nell's . . . it was perfect!

"Hello, Darien. I did it . . . bought an apartment on the East Side, for you to decorate."

"Great! Where?"

"Eighty-fourth and Third, twenty-sixth floor . . . view of Central Park and the skyline."

"What style are you thinking about for decoration?"

"A new look . . . Darien's fantasy."

"Oh . . . I can't wait . . . something of our own."

After several goodbyes, he clicked the hook to get a dial tone. The conversation with Gekko was brief and businesslike.

"Gordon, I bought an apartment on the East Side . . . $950,000, in cash."

"Terrific, Buddy . . . what's up, pal?"

"I would like to have dinner with your assistant, Alex . . . as soon as possible."

"Tonight, Bellini's at eight o'clock. Alex has been dying to show you his new brown leather Gucci attaché case."

"Thanks, Gordon . . . couldn't have done it without you."

"Nah . . . you earned it, sport. Best of luck."

Bud took a cab back to his apartment, did some paperwork, and got ready for dinner. He opened his closet, reviewed a battalion of briefcases, and selected the brown leather Gucci attaché case. Bud

glanced backward in closing the door to his apartment, like a prince regarding an animal skin he had
shed with the wave of a magic wand.

$ $ $

Harry Cipriani presided over his restaurant, much
as he had done for decades at Harry's American Bar,
his culinary institution in Venice. Diners' laughter and body language indicated that people came
here to enjoy themselves. The clientele was chic
and vigorous-looking, obviously wealthy and sportif.
It was establishment money and café society, which
seemed to have been liberated from the self-conscious
seriousness of the burghers at 21 Club.

The food was delicious: carpaccio, green ravioli,
pasta with white truffles . . . and there was much to
see. It was hard to believe that so many beautiful and
exquisitely dressed women would congregate in one
place every night.

Bud was made to feel at home, as was everyone at
Harry's place. He was escorted to Alex's table. There
was no inner circle in this small dining room. Celeb-
rities were indiscriminately scattered around the room
and at the bar; every table was thus perceived to be as
good as any other.

Bud and Alex had come with identical brown
leather Gucci attaché cases, which they placed under
the white tablecloth. After a brief dinner, both men

rose to leave. Each took the other's attaché case from beneath the table and slowly exited the restaurant in casual conversation. Buddy had acquired $950,000 in cash for his apartment.

CHAPTER XVIII

An odd procession of stock analysts, financial reporters, bankers, lawyers, and institutional shareholders defined the rolling New England countryside. The press corps grumbled its way up County Road 202 to Teldar, New Hampshire, in a yellow school bus that huffed alongside the perpetual stone fences.

A *Money Magazine* reporter yawned. "Why the hell did Cromwell call a shareholders' meeting in God's country?"

The *New York Times* financial writer laughed. "Teldar has held every annual meeting at home since 1924 . . . why change?"

"Look around you, that's why. Nobody gave a rat's ass before, but now half of Wall Street is involved in this proxy fight for control of Teldar.

Cromwell might've been decent enough to hold the vote in Manhattan."

A *Barrons* reporter jibed, "Cromwell's a dead Indian . . . burial mounds are always close to home. Gekko controls thirty-five percent of the shares. Institutions want instant gratification; balloting is a formality."

The AP correspondent disagreed. "Don't count Cromwell out. Teldar waged an effective proxy solicitation through the Carter organization . . . called every shareholder personally, twice, to tell the company's side of the story. It's not unpersuasive, if you're an investor. Management also owns three percent and controls another twenty-two through Teldar's pension fund."

A more cynical *Business Week* reporter interrupted. "Burt, how many long-term investors do you know? This is a trading market, in and out. Quick bucks today mean more than big bucks tomorrow. And how can anyone be sure that Teldar will actually realize the proffered long-term return on its assets?"

"All I'm saying is, it ain't over till the fat lady sings," replied Burt.

As they drove through the town of Teldar, its sociology was apparent. Senior management lived on the highest point in town in large, white wooden homes surrounded by several acres of manicured lawns; middle management, mill executives, and foremen were located on the second ring of the hillside in smaller homes facing neat tree-lined streets; mill hands, lumbermen, clericals, and teamsters lived in rowhouses at the base of the hill.

Many workers operated farms outside of town, normally cared for by family members. The mill arranged special hours for these workers during planting and harvest seasons, so they could sow the seeds and bring their crops in from the fields. There was also time off during hunting and fishing seasons, since Teldar folks preferred the woods and streams to the twisted trails of nearby Nashua and Boston.

G.G.'s Rolls Royce met his jet at the Nashua Airport and drove Gordon, Bud, Darien, and Harold northwest to Teldar. It was not difficult to follow the directions to the mill. As one got closer, the streams became darker from the black lignin spewed into their waters. Towering mill chimneys belched yellow sulfurous fumes into the air, which could be seen for miles around. Bad as it looked, the pollution had been much improved in the last two years by multi-million-dollar scrubbers installed to comply with mandates of the Federal Clean Air Act.

Fox pasted his nose against the car window to get his first glimpse of a paper mill—indeed of any major industrial facility.

"So this is what the fight is all about, huh, Gordon?... Wow!"

The mill dwarfed the imagination, being totally out of human scale. With one bite, monstrous cranes lifted into the air entire flatbed rail cars and truck trailers loaded with logs to apartment-building heights. Darien's mouth was open.

"Awesome . . . like lifting toys out of a neighborhood vending machine."

Raw trees were dumped from the thirty-foot heights into giant vibrators, which shook them free of debris. Massive steel belts then conveyed the timber to whizzing buzz-saw blades that cut them to uniform twelve-foot log lengths. The link belts continued their march to an automatic stripper, which peeled the bark off, then to whirling blades that sawed the logs into boards. Wood chips, bark, and other cellular waste were crushed by huge pulpers to make packaging materials.

Burly men in hard hats and earmuffs, worn to protect their eardrums from the unremitting crashing and clanging of wood and metal, guided the operations with computers and gearshifts, moving tons of machinery and timber by subtle squeezes of their fingers against delicate controls.

Men and women in overalls and jeans lined the mill gate. They stared at the suits, who gaped back at them; it was unclear who was caged. A few children threw stones at the passing convoy. One hit G.G.'s Rolls Royce. Buddy yelped.

"Those fuckin' animals."

Gekko was more sullen than anyone had seen him before. "Shut up, Fox."

Gordon felt the workers' anger but was undeterred. He was philosophically committed to attacking inefficient corporations. "Greed is good...the engine of capitalism," he comforted himself.

It was the first traffic jam in Teldar. Cars, vans, and buses choked Main Street as they unloaded their harried passengers in front of the turn-of-the-century hotel painted crimson with white trim. A narrow gray porch, occupied by rocking chairs, clung to the wooden structure.

The visitors poured through the pale-yellow foyer filled with American antiques, which had been accumulated rather than collected. Ralph Sykes, a youthful-looking merger and acquisition specialist from Anderson & Rothwell, Inc., addressed a desk clerk of similar age.

"How much would you sell that highboy for? It would do wonders for my summer home in Redding. ...Ya know"—leaning forward over the desk—"we moved and remodeled an old New England barn..."

As his astonishment subsided, the desk clerk stammered, "It's my mother's...she would never sell it."

The M&A business had taught Sykes persistence, if nothing else.

"C'mon, everything has its price. Throw out your wish-list asking price...see if I hit it."

"But, sir...it's not for sale. It belongs to my family."

"Okay, think about it...$25,000 bid...I'll be at the shareholders' meeting all day."

The American Hotel had played host to Kiwanis

Club conventions and a presidential debate during the New Hampshire primary; however, it had never received such aggressive and demanding guests. The visitors were willing to pay for everything; therefore, they assumed that anything and anyone was for sale . . . if the price was right.

Approximately four hundred people sat in folding chairs in the American Hotel ballroom, which was parted down the middle by a narrow aisle. Six young women stood in the aisle, at twenty-five-foot intervals, with hand-held microphones to facilitate shareholder questions and comments.

Self-segregation prevailed in the seating. Reporters, photographers, and TV crews occupied the first rows to the right of the aisle. Their TV lights cast an unfamiliar and eerie glow over the crowded room.

About seventy-five dark blue- and gray-suited men and women clumped together, like metallic shards in a magnetic field. Although they were outnumbered in the room, and by individual shareholders in the company, these young institutional shareholders' representatives, arbitrageurs, speculators, and securities analysts controlled Teldar's fate by virtue of the blocks of stock they would vote.

On the other side of the aisle were batteries of accountants, lawyers, bankers, and proxy solicitors, who represented opposing factions in the life-and-death struggle for corporate control; nevertheless, these professionals engaged in cheerful fraternal conversation and banter.

Retirees clustered among their relatives or in distinct generational groupings. Some had traveled great distances to stand by the company in its moment of peril . . . and to vote their small shareholdings with management.

Teldar's workers sat or stood near the back of the room. The mostly middle-aged employees were dressed in everything from undershirts to checkered sport coats. They observed in stony silence. The locals were visibly anxious about the fate of their town and livelihoods being decided by a group of alien young gunslingers.

Mr. Cromwell, a dignified sixty-year-old patrician whose family had founded Teldar, addressed the shareholders from a podium at the center of a three-tiered dais. The dais hosted thirty-three corporate officers, with titles such as Vice-President—Finance, Senior Vice-President—Operations, Vice-President—Public Relations, Group Executive Vice-President, on large place cards in front of them. Eight outside directors were present, including the chairmen of Duluth Ironworks, Royal Rubber Company, and Teldar County Bank, and a chemistry professor from Northfield University.

Cromwell recited the fiscal year results. A representative of United Arbitrage Fund asked what was on everyone's mind.

"Mr. Cromwell, sir, would you explain in more detail why Teldar lost $110 million?"

"Truly regrettable, but lumber prices were depressed due to slower housing starts . . . and Canadian producers competed through aggressive pricing in the pulp export market. Our borrowings and interest costs soared due to installations of antipollution devices under federal mandate. On a happier note, during the first two months of this fiscal year, mill prices have firmed . . . the lumber operations have returned to profitability."

Mr. Cromwell halted to formulate his thoughts on a complex matter.

"As you know, the Nashua area is one of the fastest growing high-tech regions in the United States . . . an extension of Route 128 in Massachusetts. This has been good and bad news for your company. Farmers have either refused to lease timberlands to us or are demanding exorbitant prices. In effect we are competing with real-estate developers and speculators. This hurts our bottom line. On the other hand, our owned forest lands in New Hampshire have rocketed in asset value . . . should Teldar ever decide to sell or develop all or a portion of it."

Gekko squirmed a little. This was precisely his intention. He planned to dispose of the insurance company, monetize a portion of the land through sales to real-estate developers, cut overhead at the mill operations, and sell them with the remaining timberlands to a major Canadian forest products company.

Another shareholder rose to speak. "Teldar's diversification strategy has been a disaster. What happened to our Harkum Casualty Insurance Company subsidiary?"

Cromwell sounded sad as he replied.

"We acquired Harkum three years ago. Our financial advisers recommended that we offset our total exposure to the cyclical forest products industry with an acquisition in the financial services sector. Unfortunately, the insurance cycle turned against us shortly after our purchase. We had to compete by writing policies at premiums that did not adequately compensate us for the future risks. Then Hurricane Evelyn ate up our reserves and an additional $75 million. We are more cautious about the policies that are put on the books today and have initiated talks to divest Teldar of its financial services operations."

Mr. Cromwell asked that further questions be reserved until the resolutions in the proxy material were voted on or be asked in conjunction with consideration of those resolutions. Following the balloting on reelection of auditors, he addressed the issue of "golden parachutes" for management.

"If Teldar is sold, or there is a change in a majority of its board of directors, and a member of senior management is forced to resign for any reason other than dishonesty, he would receive three years of salary."

A retiree stood up in the back and took a microphone.

"Yes, Todd?"

"Mr. Cromwell, I worked for your father . . . my son works for you. Our whole way of life is threatened if Gekko gets control of Teldar. Why should senior management receive greater protection than the working men . . . or, than all of the townspeople in Teldar? You fellows at least have stock options—we have nothing but our labor to rely on."

The audience cheered Todd Dunst. Mr. Cromwell reddened.

"Todd, I understand your point . . . share your concern for the town and its citizens; however, the realities make it necessary to protect management in order to encourage them to fight the likes of Gekko . . . without fear of losing their jobs."

A vote was called and taken. The ballots were turned over to the tallying agents.

The third resolution was addressed, the election of a board of directors. Gekko proposed a new slate of directors, in opposition to management's recommendation for the reelection of Teldar's existing board. Since major policy decisions, such as the sale of assets and the retention of management, rested with the board of directors, the future, if not the very existence of Teldar, was at stake in this vote. Cromwell was the first to speak on the resolution, from a prepared text, which he delivered with his accustomed assurance.

"Your company, ladies and gentlemen, is under siege from Gordon Gekko. Teldar Paper is now leveraged to the hilt, like some depressed South American country. Instead of using our cash to build plants, build our business, all this man really wants is to get paid to withdraw his challenge to management. *That* will cost us approximately $100 million in 'greenmail,' which will be passed on to the consumer and further leverage Teldar's balance sheet."

Gekko leaped to his feet, seething with anger.

"Where do you get off speaking about me like that? . . . I resent these remarks . . . I demand the right to speak."

Cromwell rapped his gavel on the podium.

"Sit down, sir, you're out of order. Haven't you done enough damage to Teldar as it is? Have you no sense of decency? How can your management—"

Gekko stood his ground, although Harold Solomon was urging him to be seated. Elderly retirees stood in their places shouting catcalls. "Sit down, Gekko . . ." Cromwell rapped his gavel. "Order . . . order." He picked up his prepared remarks where he had been interrupted. Cromwell was cornered and fighting mad—he feared Gekko as a businessman and despised him as a human being.

". . . concentrate on long-term growth when we're busy fighting the get-rich-quick, short-term profit, slot-machine mentality of Wall Street when we should be fighting Japan! The original, fundamental reason for Wall Street was to capitalize American business, underwrite new business, build companies, build America. The 'deal' has now succeeded goods and services as America's gross national product, and in the process, we are undermining our foundation. This cancer is called 'greed.'"

Cromwell's eyes fixed on Gekko.

"Greed and speculation have replaced long-term investment. Corporations are being taken apart like erector sets, without any consideration for the public good. I strongly recommend you to see through Mr. Gekko's shameless intentions here to strip this company and severely penalize the stockholders."

The audience was silent. Gekko squirmed, dying for a chance to be heard.

Cromwell concluded his remarks: "I strongly recommend you to reject his dissident directors' slate by voting for management's recommendations. Continuity of your board of directors will lead to a profitable restructuring, while still retaining the long-term values inherent in our forest products business."

Gekko had calmed down. As he slowly moved down the aisle in the direction of the dais, his eyes were arrested on management. He made his way from the audience to the microphone and addressed the stockholders from notes.

"I appreciate the chance you're giving me to speak, Mister Cromwell, as the single largest stockholder in Teldar."

His biting sarcasm evoked some laughter; he became looser and more strident.

"On the way here today I saw a bumper sticker. It said, 'Life's a bitch . . . and then you die!' "

Laughter was scattered in the audience.

"Well, ladies and gentlemen, we're not here to indulge in fantasies, but in political and economic reality. America has become a second-rate power. Our trade deficit and fiscal deficit are at nightmare proportions. In the days of the 'free market' when our country was a top industrial power, there was accountability to the shareholders. The Carnegies, the Mellons, the men who built this industrial empire, made sure of it because it was *their* money."

Many retirees nodded in agreement as if recalling a different time in Teldar's history.

"Today management *has no stake* in the company. Altogether these guys sitting up here own a total of less than three percent, and where does Mr. Cromwell put his million-dollar salary? Certainly not in Teldar stock—he owns less than one percent. You own Teldar, the stockholders, and *you* are being royally screwed over by these bureaucrats with their steak lunches, golf, and now golden parachutes! Teldar has thirty-three different vice-presidents, each earning over $200,000 a year. I spent two months analyzing what these guys did, and I *still* can't figure it out."

The listeners, including some of the workers, giggled knowingly. Cromwell lost his Yankee reserve.

"This is an outrage, Gekko! You're full of shit!"

Gekko had captured his audience and ignored

Cromwell, who slumped disspiritedly in his chair. Gordon continued, "One thing I do know is that Teldar lost $110 million last year, and I'd bet half of that is in paperwork going back and forth between all the vice-presidents."

There was increased laughter.

"The new law of evolution in corporate America seems to be 'survival of the unfittest!' Well, in my book, either you do it *right* or you get eliminated. Teldar is doomed to fail. Its diversification into casualty insurance has not worked. Its crown jewels are its trees, the rest is dross."

Gekko warmed to his role as an environmentalist.

"Through wars, depressions, inflation, and deterioration of paper money, trees have always kept their value, but Teldar is chopping them all down. Forests are perishable; forest rights are as important as human rights to this planet."

Gordon finally got down to his bottom line.

"All the illusory Maginot lines, scorched earth tactics, proxy fights, poison pills, et cetera, that Mr. Cromwell is going to come up with to prevent people like me from buying Teldar are doomed to fail because the bottom line, ladies and gentlemen, as *you* very well know, is that the only way to stay strong is to create value—that's why you buy stock, to have it *go up*. If there's any other reason, I've never heard of it. That's all I'm saying. . . . It's you people who own this company, *not them*—they work for you, and they've done a *lousy* job of it."

Gekko turned his back to the shareholders and pointed directly at the management.

"Get rid of them *fast*, before you all get sick and die. I may be an opportunist, but if these clowns did a better job, I'd be out of work. In the last seven deals I've been in, there were 2.3 million stockholders who actually made a pretax profit of $12 billion. When I bought the Ixtian Corporation, it was in the exact same position as Teldar is today. I let three of its companies go private into the hands of their managements, and I sold four others to companies where there were business fits—and each of these companies, liberated from the suffocating conglomerate, has *prospered*. I am not a destroyer of companies, I am a liberator of them."

Gordon felt most genuine in expressing his libertarian philosophy.

"The point is, ladies and gentlemen, *greed is good. Greed works*, greed is right. Greed clarifies, cuts through, and captures the essence of the evolutionary spirit. Greed in all its forms, greed for life, money, love, knowledge, has marked the upward surge of mankind—and greed, mark my words, will save not only Teldar but that other malfunctioning corporation called the U.S.A.... Thank you."

The suits stood up and applauded wildly. Even some of the townspeople unconsciously joined in, enthralled with the rhetoric and momentarily oblivious to their own interests; icy stares from their neighbors quickly reminded them. Cromwell had the look of a defeated man as he mechanically rapped his gavel for order.

After the ballots were counted, the corporate secretary delivered the results for each resolution. Of eighty-nine percent voting in person or by proxy:

(1 Auditors reelected: 96% for, 1% against, 3% abstentions.

(2 Management severance contracts: 32% for, 60% against, 8% abstentions.

(3 Board of Directors: Management slate 46%, Gekko slate 52%, abstentions 2%.

Darien and Buddy hugged and kissed Gordon, as countless hands reached out to congratulate him. The people of Teldar filed out without a murmur. They were in a state of shock. It was still hard for them to accept that "Mother Teldar" had been challenged, no less defeated, after almost a century of total dominance in a company town. For others, it was slowly sinking in that their way of life was just sold off on the auction block.

CHAPTER XIX

Darien spared nothing in decorating Buddy's apartment to reflect how she had always wanted to live—then she moved in.

Her decoration transformed the cookie-cutter East Side box into a sumptuous environment, evocative of ancient times. A marble floor bordered with designs of centaurs, chariots, and spear-carrying warriors greeted visitors in the foyer. Twin columns in the urban archaeology mode announced entry to the living room, which was now separated from the dining room by an eliptical wall. New moldings added shape and warmth to the place.

Several young artists whom Darien knew from SoHo painted a neoclassical mural on the long side of the living room. A large antique sideboard with a fitted brass sink decorated the opposite wall and served as a bar. An enormous sofa encased in an ecru linen slipcover, made deliberately baggy and tied on with rows of self-bows on each end, filled the center of the room. Several Etruscan pots wired up as lamps, and a poured concrete coffee table that looked as if it had survived Pompeii, nourished the atmosphere. The bleached living-room floor was mostly covered with a hand-painted floor cloth, instead of a rug, which revealed carefully stenciled ancient patterns on its exposed portions.

The kitchen was ultramodern, where the compact computer was king. Buddy's daily domestic life was ruled by computerized telephones, lights, dishwasher, microwave, garbage compactor, vinaigrette mixer, and stereo . . . Bud needed a manual just to play a Duran Duran album.

The bedroom held a short, squat bed with a stone Roman storage bin at its foot. Two decapitated Ionian columns balanced a heavy glass top to form the dressing table. Venetian glassware and antique vases were displayed in a vitrine; a terra cotta pot with a spray of flowers occupied its counterpart on the other side of the window.

Months of decorating yielded no prospect of an early end to it, although Bud had considered the apartment complete long ago. He was uneasy with the growing pile of bills, as well as with the constant intrusions on his sensibilities and privacy.

Darien was lying on the bed after they had finished making love. Bud took the occasion to express his concerns.

"You know, the elevator man couldn't believe I paid $300,000 to have my walls looking like this— he got them for free in Brooklyn."

She was stung.

"I'll bet he has an opinion on the stock market, too. This apartment is already ahead of its time. I call it the demolished look! They've already heard about it at *House and Garden;* they're coming to photograph it next week, before it gets too . . . lived in. It's ideal for my portfolio."

What had started out between *them* as "Darien's fantasy" to live in was now the "demolished look" so that magazine readers could have a catchy phrase to throw around on the cocktail-party circuit.

"Does helping your portfolio earn me a discount? Considering we're way over budget, your fee should be negotiable . . . ?"

Darien seemed defensive at first, but this quickly turned to aggression.

"Let's get things straight, Bud. I'm not going to take a cut. I worked hard, and you *can't* decorate a room in New York for less than $100,000. Curtains alone . . ."

Bud interrupted, as he left the bedroom waving

his hands above his head, "I'm kidding, I'm kidding. . . . So what's money anyway when everybody's making it . . . it's all relative!"

Bud stepped out on the balcony to cool off. He looked back through the glass door at the bedroom and Darien, momentarily locked in thought. The room was exquisite in its restrained elegance. Perfect, yet untouchable—like Darien, making love with her laid-back receptivity, a nineteenth century Victorian woman's "do with me as you will" attitude. Darien was beautiful to behold, but as nonparticipatory in bed as the ancient stone that surrounded her.

Bud was in awe of Darien and his apartment, but uncomfortable with both. He turned toward the night, New York with all of its glittering promise. Bud looked vacantly into himself.

"Who am I . . . ?"

Feelings hurt too much. His mind would not permit him to go further. He concluded quickly that he had everything: money, a magnificent girl, an extraordinary apartment. Bud was a perfect 10! *So what's there to worry about? It was time to get back to work; make some money to pay for these wonders,* he thought.

Bud telephoned his broker in Hong Kong.

"Buy gold . . . 250 ounces of bullion at $454. . . . Convert the bonds . . . but only after checking the prices in Tokyo. What's your number one idea? . . .

no . . . I'll wait for a sure thing. I get a hundred ideas a day . . . mostly crap."

Bud put down the receiver.

I need a big idea to launch me into Gekko's stratosphere, he thought.

$ $ $

Bud knew he had to initiate his own deal. He kept thinking about the hidden assets that had made the Teldar takeover work. If only he could find another Teldar . . .

He sat down at his computer and did screens of potential targets. Image after image flashed before him. Hour after hour passed by, but nothing leaped out. Determined but exhausted, Buddy plugged away.

Finally, something appeared on the screen that blew his mind — the corporate profile of Bluestar Airlines. *Of course,* Buddy thought, *it's perfect!*

$ $ $

Bud went on to devise a plan that would bring him riches and respectability. As the early morning hours approached, he woke Darien to share his brainstorm.

"Darien, I'm a genius . . . lightning has struck."

She rolled over on her side.

"Did you stay up all night again? Y'ever hear of the sixty-hour work week? You're turning into a yuppie Frankenstein, you love money so much."

"Sure, why not, money's the sex of the eighties.

Money's as serious as a heart attack. Darien, you've gotta listen to this."

He spit out his ideas in rapid-fire succession to a half-asleep interior decorator and ended with part prediction, part plea.

"You think I'm gonna be a broker the rest of my life? This will make me an entrepreneur . . . I'll be a giant in business."

As Darien fell back asleep, she mumbled, "Be anything you want . . . but don't be naive."

$ $ $

That morning Buddy invited himself aboard Gekko's jet for a business trip to Chicago, in order to make his presentation to a captive audience. Fox rehearsed the major points, as G.G.'s Gulfstream banked toward the sky.

The target company's assets were adequate to finance its own takeover; nevertheless, its stock price was low because operating losses generated insufficient cash flow to repay principal and interest in a leveraged buyout. Fox controlled the key human ingredients to transform those losses into profits.

Gekko was patting the pretty French stewardess on her behind as she smilingly served the gentlemen Tattinger's champagne and Iranian caviar. Buddy popped the proposal.

"Bluestar's an unpolished gem, Gordon. A half-assed management is being decimated by a price war it launched and cannot win. But the assets . . . the landing slots and gates at La Guardia alone are worth twenty-five dollars a share if they're worth a dime! It's ripe to fall into our hands."

Gekko had a poker face, waiting for Buddy to show more cards.

"Mixed emotions, Buddy. Men as smart as myself have got their asses handed to them with the airlines. Fuel could go up, unions are killers . . ."

"Yeah, but aren't you forgetting something, Gordon? Rule one: capital reserves. This company has $75 million *cash* in an overfunded pension. That buys a lot of credibility at the bank."

Gekko's interest was piqued. Alex interrupted with a shout from the rear of the plane, his hand over the telephone mouthpiece.

"Gordon, the insurance people are balking on the logging trucks . . ."

"Tell those spineless toads we'll self-insure, if they don't write it . . ." He turned to Buddy. "I fired thirty-three officers and two hundred and fifty employees at Teldar and nothing has changed."

Gordon looked at Buddy suspiciously. "You're tense, pal. What do you *really* want out of this Bluestar deal?"

Fox's eyes narrowed in their sockets, as if to signal that the ante had been raised.

"Gordon, what I want—and I never asked you for anything—is to be your copilot on this. I want to take this airline, turn it around, and make it work. I'll make us a fortune."

Gekko's right index finger tapped his temple to indicate he was experiencing brain damage.

"I'm talking to a stockbroker who wants to run an airline . . . with my money riding on it. It's gonna take me two years and two thousand headaches to turn Teldar Paper around . . . what do I need this dink airline for? I'm up to my ass in more nuts than a fruitcake."

"Gordon, I worked at Bluestar, I know my way around, I have friends there . . . inside."

Gekko's broadly amused smile narrowed into newly found concentration when he caught the drift that there might be an inside track here.

"What does that mean?"

Buddy played his next card. He spoke slowly and methodically, with the confidence of a Louisiana politician.

"The three unions . . . labor is forty-three percent of Bluestar's operating budget—the hourly cost of a flight crew is $850; there's the real potential value. If we can negotiate that out, get a crew down to $350, 400 an hour per run, this airline would be hotter than Texas Air . . . a cash machine."

Gekko crossed into the realm of high seriousness.

"What makes you think you can get labor concessions?"

Buddy turned up his ace in the hole.

"I can talk to these people, Gordon, they trust me . . . and my father can be a big help in getting cuts."

Gekko pursed his lips in a maybe-you-got-something gesture. He turned to his secretary.

"All right, get Buckingham on the box. I want him to analyze Bluestar . . . and tell Jack Taylor at Thwick, Jensen to check out the legal."

Gekko smiled wickedly at Fox — a devil's disciple expression of one who has looked into a mirror and seen himself transparently.

"So, sport, the falcon has heard the falconer."

$ $ $

Fox scheduled a meeting between Gekko and the union leaders to win their assent to his plan. He concluded that Bluestar was mired in financial trouble because its equipment expansion and fare discounts went far enough to be costly without being sufficiently aggressive to really challenge the majors. His approach, he believed, would accomplish all of his desires in one fell swoop. Bud would be a hero with his family's lifetime friends and neighbors by averting the threatened layoffs, while reaping financial rewards and recognition as a top-notch airline chieftain. What could be more perfect than good deeds and personal gain wrapped in one package, he thought.

Toni Carpenter, representative of the Association of Flight Attendants, was the first to arrive at Buddy's apartment building for a meeting between Gekko and Bluestar's labor leaders. She opened her purse in the elevator and juggled a mirror, compact, and lipstick to apply the finishing touches.

Bud introduced himself to the attractive fortyishlooking woman at the door. Toni stood ramrod straight and had the ready smile of someone used to serving others; she also had the tough-minded resourcefulness characteristic of veteran stewardesses on business flights.

Duncan Wilmore, a seasoned pilot, spoke for the Airline Pilot's Association; he arrived in a neatly pressed uniform, accompanied by Al Tatum, leader of the Baggage Handler's Union. Tatum wore a woolen cap and a dark blue pea jacket over a red-checked flannel shirt that uneasily contained "Big Al's" overflow of fat and muscle.

Darien greeted them at the door in a black strapless silk dress that pinched and tucked in just the right places; her blond hair flowed gracefully over her naked shoulders. The picture window behind Darien framed falling snowflakes, dissolving the city's night lights and softening New York's skyline.

Big Al leaned his head over to Duncan. "Holy shit!"

Darien was an exclamation point for all that Buddy had acquired. Al was prepared to accept the fantasy world of the Rockefellers and the Mellons, even the suburban mansions of airline moguls, but he couldn't absorb Carl Fox's romantic boy living in a Greek revival palace in the heart of Manhattan. He wondered what it was like to have the perfect blond mistress in silk, instead of catching nookie from waitresses in cheap motels. A life where bills didn't matter and you could skip shopping for specials; where

you didn't have to creep along the Belt Parkway from
Brooklyn to work . . . from work to Brooklyn.

The unionists clustered together on the massive
ecru couch, exhibiting the uncertain courage of
people who faced forces that they consider overwhelming. These men and women shouldered
responsibilities for thousands of families. They were
afraid to go down a dark unmarked road, on a blind
date with "Gekko the Great," ruthless rapist of companies. Their hearts beat fast, their minds ran in different directions—*even a predator is unpredictable
and may do good under certain circumstances . . .
hope is an addiction . . . Gekko is a deceitful dog. . . .*

Darien served drinks and canapés. Bud tried to put
everyone at ease with light conversation and an inspection of his stereo equipment

The room quieted abruptly as persistent doorbell
ringing sent a quiver through the apartment. Darien
opened the door and welcomed Carl Fox with her
cheeriest campus-queen smile. Carl stood in the
foyer, his hair laced with wet snow. He refused to
surrender his leather bomber jacket as Darien
escorted him into the living room. Buddy hugged his
father.

"Dad, well come on in. Everybody's here. We
couldn't start the show without you."

Carl's eyes swooped around the living room, like
swallows searching for insects. He mumbled under
his breath, "Well, I'll be a lousy Republican."

Darien overheard. "I decorate for Democrats, too, lots of them. I live here with your son."

"I know. You're one of the art works that go with the apartment." Carl softened a little. "Pretty creative. Doesn't look anything like the apartment my son bought a few months ago."

"Listen, I hope you'll come here often, and under less formal circumstances," Darien replied half-apologetically.

Buddy took Carl by the arm.

"Dad, you know Duncan Wilmore, pilots' union, Toni Carpenter, flight attendants, and Al Tatum, baggage handlers . . ."

Carl nodded to them familiarly.

"I met them before you were born."

"And I'd like to introduce Mr. Gekko and his lawyer, Mr. Solomon."

Gordon extended his hand in warm greeting, as if to a friend or relative. "Pleased to meet you, Mr. Fox."

Carl didn't budge, as he probed the face of the man who had stolen his son's affection. He wanted a clue to justify the decision he had already made deep down—he would have nothing to do with Gordon Gekko. Carl would listen, watch, and wait for an opportunity to undo his rival. He would prove to his son that wealth had not mellowed the evil that had seduced him.

"I thought this was an informal meeting. What's he doing here?" He pointed toward Harold Solomon.

Gekko smiled compliantly. "Harold, you don't mind strolling around the block a couple of hundred times, do you?"

"Of course," Solomon replied obediently, as he theatrically glanced at his watch and left.

Carl and Gordon eyed one another, tentatively. Gekko decided on the spot to address the union leaders without delay, sensing that any hesitation would result in further deterioration of the atmosphere.

"Look, I have no illusions about winning a popularity contest with any of you. I was roasted the other night, and a friend of mine asked, 'Why are we honoring this man—have we run out of human beings?'"

Gekko's self-deprecation broke the ice. Everyone laughed, with the exception of Carl. Gordon continued his presentation, in the tone of a teacher.

Toni Carpenter took notes in her small red diary.

"It's not always the most popular guy who gets the job done. You got losses of twenty to thirty million dollars, dividends cut to zero, you're getting squeezed to death by the majors. Present management may not be the worst scum of the earth, but they're the ones who've put you on a kamikaze course, and pretty soon everybody's going to be scrambling for the parachutes. Only there aren't enough to go around. Management has them. You don't."

Carl Fox made loud crunching noises as he bit into

a carrot and chewed. He glared unrepentantly at Gekko.

"If they throw Bluestar into Chapter Eleven— which I think they will—then they can use bankruptcy laws to break your unions and your contracts and throw you guys off the property."

"With all due respect, Mr. Gekko," asked Duncan Wilmore, "what's to prevent you from doing the same thing?"

Gordon was prepared.

" 'Cause I have a way around all this, a way we can all make money and make this airline profitable again. What do you say we cut to the chase? I'm asking for a modest twenty percent across-the-board wage cut."

Carl's glass clunked on the table, as Gekko continued unfazed.

"And seven more hours a month."

The union officials exchanged skeptical glances, but Gekko was encouraged when Toni Carpenter pressed for more details, rather than waving goodbye.

"What kind of time frame are we talking about here?"

Gordon was determined not to lose the opening. He paused for a moment. His body language indicated an "I'll put my feet to the fire" conclusion.

"Give me a year. If we're still losing money, the reductions stand. If, however, we move into the black, I return part of the givebacks, salaries go back to present levels, and . . . we institute an employee profit-sharing program with stock. You'll own part of the airline."

The unionists were surprised by his offer of an equity participation in the airline. Gekko steered them, like a child with a toy car. They desperately wanted to believe that there was a neat solution to Bluestar's problems. Buddy saw the initiative shift to Gordon. He smiled smugly at Darien, although he was puzzled by his father's silence.

Carl watched his colleagues being seduced by the devil. Something froze inside of him. For the first time, he was afraid of Gordon Gekko.

Duncan asked, "Are you prepared to put your promises in writing?"

Gekko responded in a voice overflowing with sincerity. "I'll have a letter-agreement drawn up within two days."

Toni viewed Gordon's proposition as flawless from a distance, but sparse on specifics.

"What's your marketing strategy? How do you plan to return us to profitability?"

Carl was staggered by his colleagues' willingness to accept the illusion of recovery, proffered by someone whose only claim to fame was shuffling paper among corporations. His face was overcast with frustration. *Snake oil is always more popular than the arduous cure dictated by reality,* Carl thought. Gordon picked up on the sentiment and acted to deflect it.

"Why don't I give Buddy an opportunity to answer the questions about marketing strategy and profitability."

Carl moved to the edge of his armchair, ashamed to see his son so ruthlessly manipulated.

Bud came forward. Carl noticed he had become slightly plump. Young eyes were set in fleshy pouches; there was a new softness around his middle. A countervailing hardness had seized Bud's spirit. He spoke as if possessed by a dybbuk. Buddy was a convert and made you want to believe him. The group followed him with telescopic fixation when he paced the living room.

"Thank you, Mr. Gekko. First of all I want you to know my door will always be open to you, 'cause I know from my dad that it's you guys who keep Bluestar flying. We must act immediately to save the airline and *our* jobs. One—modernize. Our computer software is weak; we update it and squeeze every dollar out of each seat and mile flown. You don't sell a seat to a guy for $89 when he's willing to pay $389. Effective inventory management through computerization will increase our load factor by five to twenty percent, which translates to approximately $50 to $200 million in revenues. The point is, we can beat the giant carriers by being more efficient. Two —advertising. More—more and aggressive . . . attack the big boys. Three—expand our hubs to Atlanta, North Carolina, and Dallas, reorganize all our feeder schedules, think *big*, guys, 'cause we're going after the majors."

Bud's determination was contagious. Gekko rode the crest of his zealotry.

"Cards are on the table. What do you think?"

Duncan Wilmore was restrained, but hopeful. "If you mean what you say, I think we're in the ball park. I'll take it to my people."

Toni Carpenter checked her notes before she responded. "You've sketched some broad strokes. I'd like to see the fine print. But so far so good."

Big Al nodded his acquiescence.

Bud tensed. All eyes had turned to Carl Fox, who broke his silence.

"I guess if a man lives long enough, he gets to see *everything*. What else do you have in your bag of tricks, Mr. Gekko?"

Gordon was close to getting what he wanted. He ignored the innuendo with finesse.

"Frankly, Carl, I can't see giving much more. If you have any suggestions, I'll be glad to listen."

Carl had miles of misgivings, but how could he explain them when he was numbed by the sight of his son as a slave?

"As the Bible says, 'There came into Egypt a Pharoah who did not know.'"

"I beg your pardon? Is that a proverb?" Gekko smiled politely.

"No, it's a prophecy. The rich have been doing it to the poor since the beginning of time. The only difference between the pyramids and the Empire State Building is that the Egyptians didn't have unions." He stared straight at his couinionists. "I know what this guy is about—greed—he's in and out for the buck and he don't take prisoners. He don't give a damn about Bluestar, or us."

"Now, wait a minute, Dad . . ." Bud tried to cloak his panic with assertiveness. Gekko interrupted him.

"Sure. What's worth doing is worth doing for money. It's a bad bargain where nobody gains, but if this deal goes through, we *all* gain."

Carl threw his napkin on the floor and rose from the armchair. He looked aged and menacing. His voice was seeping with cynicism.

"Of course my son did work three summers as a baggage handler and freight loader. With those qualifications, why should I doubt his ability to run an airline?"

"Fine," said Gekko with a shrug. "If you don't want us, stay with the scum in present management —dedicated to running you and Bluestar into the ground."

Carl Fox was outraged by the notion that the life of his company was being squeezed into dead numbers by armchair generals. He exploded.

"That 'scum' built this company up from one plane in thirty years; they made something out of nothing while you were skimming rents from poor people in Brooklyn. . . . If that's scum, I'll take it over a rat any day."

There was frozen silence. Carl grieved to feel isolated in his own son's home...among his co-workers. He waved his hand in finale, declared, "I'm gone," and closed the door behind him.

Gekko hissed in anger, "Even fathers become traitors." Bud ran into the hallway after his dad, reaching him at the elevator. He pounded Carl's shoulders with his fists, like a frustrated four-year-old.

"Congratulations. You did a great job of embarrassing me in there—not to mention yourself! Save the 'workers of the world, unite' speech for next time, Dad, I heard it too much growing up. You're gonna get axed, Dad, no two ways about it. You and the airline are going down the tubes, you hear me? Just like Braniff. You don't have a chance in hell, and if it isn't Gekko, it's gonna be some other killer."

The elevator door opened. Both men slumped against the back of the empty car. An odd couple, they looked alike, except two decades apart—Bud sweating in his Giorgio Armani suit, Carl steaming in his bomber jacket. Carl was being destroyed by what could not be seen inside Buddy's Armani suit.

"He's got your prick in his back pocket, son, and you're standing naked in the display window of Macy's. He's using you. Only you're too blind to see it."

Bud went for the jugular.

"No, what I see is a jealous old machinist who can't stand that his son's become more successful than himself."

195

"What you see, son, is a man who never measured success by the size of a man's wallet."

Nature's unresolved conflicts had taken command.

"That's because you never had the guts to go out into the world and stake your claim."

Fatigue overcame outrage; Carl's facial expression slackened.

"Boy, if that's what you think, I must've really screwed up my job as a father."

They emerged from the elevator, locked in the moment, oblivious to others in the lobby.

"As far as being axed, I'm still here, and as long as I am, I have a responsibility not just to me but to the union members I represent."

Buddy's aggression turned to cajoling. "Your responsibility, Dad, is to present the *facts*, not your opinions, to the men. . . . You're gonna destroy their lives, Dad! Don't do it to 'em. Give it a chance. Let the membership decide for itself, Dad. *Please*."

"I'll be damned if, when my men come to me tomorrow morning, wanting to know what's going on, I'm going to lie to them!"

"Your men! All my life 'your men' have been able to count on you. Why is it that you've never been there for me?" Carl's self-righteousness was infuriating, and Buddy continued his attack. "And what if you're wrong? What if one day the sun didn't rise in the east and birds didn't fly south in the winter and for once in your life your compass was off? Huh?"

The snow was falling as the conversation spilled

into the street. Snowflakes provided a natural shield against the city, temporarily eclipsing its dark heart. Bud grabbed his father by the arm. He was desperate, tears welling in his eyes. Pleading!

"You owe me one chance, Dad. I wasn't born with a silver spoon in my mouth. I fuckin' scraped my knees for everything at Jackson & Steinhem. Would you be willing to wreck my future? Your men's future? Think! Be practical, for a change. I'm asking you, I'm fucking begging you . . ."

Carl stared at the janitors wielding shovels, turning snowflakes into slush, and at his son, a grotesque figure begging in the snow to fulfill his outsized ambition.

"I don't sleep with no whore and I don't wake up with no whore. That's how I live with myself, Buddy. I don't know how you do. I hope I'm wrong. I'll let the men decide for themselves, that much I promise you."

Buddy watched his father stagger off into the distance through the snow—New York's nighttime architecture, outrage bowed by weariness. And all Buddy could think of was that he had won the deal.

CHAPTER XX

Buddy's youthful egocentrism was so busy *willing* what he wanted to happen into reality that his senses were dulled to the objective dangers surrounding him. Fox's ambition refused to be distracted by people or events that didn't fit into his prospectus.

The grave young man who had been the SEC investigator assigned to Teldar at the New York Stock Exchange Stock Watch Office entered his bureau chief's room carrying a thick file. Harry Hawkins's divinity school education had given him a universal framework of rights and wrongs by which to judge everyday conduct, and he was not easily swayed from his course. Being about the same age as Buddy, experience with people and the harsh realities of life had not yet mellowed his illusions about what "ought to be." Harry lived in moral isolation from the people he was regulating. He could not even understand their tireless pursuit of money, which he found tiresome.

Mickey Morgenstein's large office was dark except for a fluorescent desk lamp. The smell of pipe tobacco filled the air. A heavy wooden table stood against one wall and an old leather couch crowded the other. Both were piled high with open law books, thick legal briefs, newspaper clippings, journals, and mountains of unidentified debris. It looked like things were only added to the cache, never removed. Mickey's walls were covered with degrees, awards, and photos of its occupant with prominent people. Despite this menagerie, he always felt deprived of adequate recognition for his long career in government service.

Morgenstein had large lips and jowly cheeks, with an ample nose splashing over them. Heavy-framed glasses made his brown eyes seem small and suspicious. He was a well-known figure in the bar association and law review circuits, enjoying nothing more than to lecture the private bar on the subtleties of his legal interpretations. Indeed, some said he sought to take on complex and esoteric cases so that they would lead inevitably to such invitations.

Morgenstein was forty-four and had two children about to enter college. He was secretly hoping to convert from government prosecutor to defense attorney with a fat paycheck from a Washington or Wall Street law firm. He could not help thinking that a few big courtroom victories over leading corporations might facilitate that transition.

Mickey motioned for Hawkins to sit down. Two hard-backed chairs stood in eerie isolation before Morgenstein's dimly lit worn, wooden desk. As always, few words were exchanged between these two men.

"It's slow going on the Teldar investigation. The buyers are scattered, mostly small foreign brokers and corporations over whom the SEC has no jurisdiction."

Morgenstein's eyelids drooped, as if a familiar, albeit not fruitful, conversation were about to take place.

"Don't waste your time on an insider trading case. I have complicated issues of law that need to be investigated."

Harry was stern, the vicar of the faith.

"My gut tells me there's a conspiracy here. I hate this cheap philosophy that money is God. Everything goes in getting it . . . destroys the purity of the marketplace."

Mickey always sounded tense when he spoke. He leaned across the desk, looking straight into his listener's face, to make an ordinary statement seem like a papal pronouncement.

"Look, it will be a tedious investigation. Insider trading is difficult to prove with such elusive issues as intent, state of mind, and causation . . . and if you crack the sonofabitch, it still gets you nothing. Forget it!"

Harry was a hard-boiled individualist; his determination was clear as he got up to leave the room.

"I have a lead to follow. Some guy in Aspen bought 200,000 shares of Teldar."

$ $ $

Dixon Bates was generally in a state of permanent excitement. Nevertheless, his speech was particularly slovenly as he screamed into the phone at Buddy in his office.

"Calm down, Dixon! What are you talking about?"

"This guy who said he was from the Securities Exchange Commission, whatever the hell that is, calls and wants to ask me about that stock I bought . . ."

Fox had a vacant look in his eyes. "What'd you tell him?"

Dixon sounded bewildered. "I told him I was in the bathroom and I'd call him right back. What the hell was I supposed to say? Buddy, you got me into—"

Bud responded matter-of-factly. "Look, Dixon, calm down. It's not illegal to buy stock or to be right.

202

And it's not all that unusual to be spot-checked on a big buy. Tell him you did your homework and you thought the stock was a sound investment. Not one word more than that."

Dixon was nervous as a kitten. "What if they don't believe me?"

"They will."

"You sure?"

"Yes. Read the Constitution, it's all in there. And remember—you don't know anything, nothing."

Bates sounded relieved, but skeptical. "I *don't* know anything!"

"Good. Then call him back. And call me back. Don't worry."

$ $ $

Bud's secretary put through a call from Roger Barnes. He had urgent business to discuss, which could not be dealt with on the telephone. Fox left Jackson & Steinhem in a hurry and took a Dial-a-Cab uptown to Botts, Barnes & Dorrance. Buddy had an absent, preoccupied expression when he entered Roger's office.

"So what's the problem?"

Barnes was very nervous. "Got a strange call from the SEC. They asked to see my records. Buddy, this is a heavy—"

Fox shrugged with reassuring confidence. "Relax, Roger. You're M82 in a Swiss numbered account, and I'm the Invisible Man. They're always looking for red flags — my friends are always getting checked by them; they never come up with anything . . . we're invulnerable on this."

Roger added, somewhat mystified, "This SEC investigator asked me if I knew Dixon Bates in college, of all things."

Was everything breaking down, flying out of control? Fox wondered with a shudder.

"What did you say?"

"The truth. I hardly knew him . . . he was a year behind me, and I haven't seen him since graduation."

Roger paused and added, "I just wanna slow down, Buddy . . . no more calls for a while, no more lunches. . . . We suspend our partnership, all right?"

"Sure, Roger, whatever you want; it's cool."

A young lawyer, with his shirt-sleeves rolled up and tie hanging down at the third button of his creased white shirt, popped his head into Roger's office.

"Rog, come on . . . it's started."

Roger threw back his head in fatigue, as he and Buddy left the office.

"Since Gekko asked us into the Bluestar deal, we've been working around the clock. After an all-nighter, we're finally ready to review the timetable . . . wanna come?"

Buddy's expression betrayed surprise. "He never told me . . ."

Roger responded half-mockingly, "You're just the president of the company. What do you know?"

$ $ $

Buddy and Roger entered a large conference room. A highly polished, huge wooden table occupied the center of the room, resting on a blue and red Persian carpet. Straight-backed red-velvet cushioned chairs lined the paneled walls, standing under the portraits of six generations of senior partners. The outer wall provided a panoramic view of New York through uninterrupted floor-to-ceiling windows.

Despite the severe-looking portraits around the room, the people now most honored at Botts, Barnes & Dorrance were financial craftsmen, not legal scholars. The conference-room table was well equipped with the devices of modern corporate warfare: desktop and portable computers, Hewlitt-Packard calculators, audio-visual equipment, and ubiquitous Merlin telephone sets. The remnants of Chinese noodles, cold pizza slices, crushed soda cans, coffee containers, danishes, and bagels and cream cheese were littered among the high-tech equipment, artifacts of human interaction with this semiconductor warfare.

The air smelled vaguely of sweat and anxiety. The professions—lawyers, investment bankers, accountants, and commercial bankers—were each represented by a partner and two associates. All of the

205

action in the world was centered in this room, as far as the group was concerned, as the experts expended their peak life energies in blind ardor for *the deal*. Roger interrupted to introduce Bud.

"You guys know the new chief of Bluestar, Bud Fox."

The assemblage nodded disinterestedly, reflecting their recognition of Fox's figurehead status.

Bud tensed slightly to see Bluestar being dissected before strangers in cold calculations on the screen. An arrow from a searchlight pointer, operated by a young investment banking associate, scored his boss's presentation with visual detail. The arrow was on a footnote that indicated a $75 million overfunded pension plan.

Fox recognized the partner from New World Securities Inc., the hottest deal-firm on Wall Street. Jeff Burnside was rubbing his hands like a glutton in a children's fairy tale as he described the Bluestar takeover strategy.

Burnside was an ugly customer; red suspenders battled his business-lunch bulge, and a beaked nose drooped over his vibrating lips. He drove every point home with angry force, whether or not force was required. After outlining the attack on Bluestar, the new-breed investment banker suddenly turned on the stuffier commercial bankers, accusing them of withholding timely logistical support.

"Look, guys, what's the problem, let's go for the kill. Gekko's got twelve percent and climbing, plus the unions are in his pocket for now. Everybody on the Street knows the stock's in play."

His associate interjected, "Up two and a quarter since the opening."

Burnside continued his harangue with aggressively narrowed eyes. "By next week, the Street's gonna own Bluestar, and management will be under enormous pressure to make a deal. *Why are you guys dicking around?*"

Burnside's expression was mean and crude. The commercial bankers thought Burnside was a throwback to the Middle Ages, when he would have delighted in administering the rack, thumbscrews, and brand to get his way. He had even boasted earlier in the meeting that his tactics had once caused a protagonist to have a heart attack at the negotiating table. Burnside's continued hammering sent a chill through his audience.

"Is the bank financing in place or are we gonna have more and more meetings? Our firm's gonna guarantee twenty-five percent of the total debt structure in long-term junk bonds. Your banks loan billions to Wasi Wasiland without batting an eyelash, so what's your problem with a real credit? Now you guys either sign this piece of paper right now, or we're gonna pull and head for another bank group for the short-term money. . . ."

The commercial bankers cultivated respectability, often in lieu of the higher compensation packages earned by their more dynamic investment banking counterparts. They responded to Burnside's loud threats with low-key appeasement.

"Look, we have thirty banks ready to participate in a four-year revolving credit line, but we *have* to have your written assurance to pay back most of the money loaned in the first six months, and the only way—"

Burnside cut him off jeeringly: "Thirty banks, isn't that wonderful . . . You got it, no problem."

The commercial bankers suppressed their unspeakable disgust with Burnside to protect their fee. They soberly insisted on their lending conditions.

"And the only way we can see this happening is by liquidating the hangars and the planes. Can you people guarantee that? We're only making a bridge loan?"

The inevitability of disaster gripped Buddy's stomach like a tick when he heard the word *liquidate*. He felt solitary in his terror and humiliation. Bud turned his eyes upon himself and looked at his body as if he were filthy. Was his father right after all? Betrayal and disintegration hung in the air like a dark cloud before Buddy's eyes, as Burnside answered the bankers.

"Guaranteed! No sweat . . . we already got the Bleezer brothers lined up to build condos where the hangars are. We can lay off the planes with Mexicano. Midcontinental Air is drooling to get the slots and routes. What's the problem? It's done."

Barnes passed a formal-looking spreadsheet to the commercial bankers.

"This is the price tag on the 737s, the gates, the hangars, the routes. . . . We got it all nailed down to the typewriters."

Torment, shame, and self-mockery exploded inside Buddy like a cancer. *So this was hell*, he thought. Burnside's voice sounded distorted to him in the background as he detailed the dismemberment of Bluestar.

"The beauty of it is the overfunded pension fund. Gekko gets the seventy-five million in there. Fifty million buys him the minimum annuities' protection for six thousand employees, and he walks away with the rest. All in, he'll net sixty to seventy million. Not bad for a month's work." He turned to Buddy. "Your man did his homework, Fox . . . you're gonna have a short executive career. Now he'll really start believing he's Gekko the Great!"

$ $ $

Bud walked out of the conference room in suffering and self-derision, feeling he had violated the taboos against patricide, betrayal of friends, lying, and greed. The approaching business and personal catastrophes made his adrenaline rush to meet the terror, as he charged through Gekko's waiting room.

Natalie was on the phone as Buddy flashed by her desk. She cupped the receiver and whispered, "Buddy, you can't go in there. He's in a meeting!"

Fox ignored her and flung open Gekko's door. Gordon was talking with a senior Japanese delegation; he tossed his head around to repel Bud's intrusion.

"I didn't know we had a meeting scheduled for this morning."

"I'm sorry, this can't wait."

Gekko planted a piercing stare on Bud.

"Will you gentlemen excuse us?"

They bowed and left discreetly. As the door closed behind them, Gordon turned his full anger on Fox.

"What the hell do you want?"

Hurt laced Buddy's voice. "I found out about the garage sale at Bluestar. Why?"

Gekko took on the air of a general being questioned by a private.

"Last night I read my son the story of Winnie the Pooh and the Honey Pot. Know what happened? He stuck his nose in that honey pot once too often and got stung."

"Maybe you ought to read him Pinocchio. You told me you were going to turn Bluestar around . . . not upside down. You used me."

"You're walking around blind without a cane, sport. A fool and his money are lucky to get together in the first place," Gekko said stingingly.

"Why do you need to wreck this company?"

"Because it's wreckable. I took another look, and I changed my mind."

Buddy put the palm of his hand against his brow in despair. "If these people lose their jobs, there's nowhere for them to go. My father's worked at Bluestar for twenty-four years. I gave them my word."

Gekko's tone was as hard and cold as an ice block. "It's all about bucks, kid, the rest is conversation." Gekko lightened up for a moment. "Bud, you're still going to be president. And when the time comes, you'll parachute out a rich man. With the money you're going to make, your father won't have to work another day in his life."

Bud was no longer capable of confusing his standards by surgically separating "them" from "us."

"Tell me, Gordon—when does it all end? How many yachts can you water-ski behind? How much is enough?"

The icy tone in Gekko's voice returned. "Buddy, it's not a question of enough. It's a zero-sum game, sport. Somebody wins and somebody loses. Money itself isn't lost or made, it's simply *transferred* from one perception to another. Like magic. That painting"—he pointed—"cost $60,000 ten years ago. I could sell it for $600,000. The illusion has become real! And the more real it becomes, the more desperately they want it. Capitalism at its finest."

Buddy pounded the table with his fist as he paced past it. "I said, how much is enough, Gordon?"

"Life is not about limits. We make the rules, Buddy . . . the news, war, peace, famine, upheaval—

the cost of a paper clip. We pull the rabbit out of the hat, while everybody else sits around their whole life wondering how we did it. I create *nothing; I own!*"

Gekko crossed over to Buddy and put his arm on his shoulders.

"You're not vain enough to think we're living in a democracy, are you, Buddy? It's the free market. You're one of us now . . . take advantage of it. You got the killer instinct, kid, stick with me. I got things to teach you."

"Obviously . . ."

Gordon led Bud to the door consolingly. "Believe me, Buddy, I was gonna discuss this with you at the right time. Look, why don't you calm down and come to the apartment for dinner tonight. Bring Darien."

"I can't make it tonight," Fox stammered.

Gekko stopped Bud at the door, his arm around his shoulders.

"Are you with me, Buddy?" When there was no reply, Gekko tightened his grip on Bud's left shoulder muscle; a look of unmistakable power—and danger —was written in every aspect of Gekko's person in the doorway.

"I want you with me." He waited for an answer.

"I'm with you, Gordon."

When Bud was gone, Gekko reached for a telephone in controlled rage.

"This is Gordon Gekko. Now I want ziplocked

mouths on Bluestar, or I'm gonna personally come down there and rip out your fucking throats!"

$ $ $

Darien stiffened with dread at the sight of Ionian columns, classical vases, and antique glass smashed on her living-room floor. Buddy's head hung over the couch arm, his eyes rolling bewilderedly in their sockets. He clutched an empty bottle of tequila.

Fox felt like an autoimmune boy in a bubble, the inevitable forces of his destruction everywhere about him. Inner torture was intensified by growing self-awareness of his role in teeing up the impending Bluestar tragedy. He was bitter that his friend and mentor had betrayed him, but more painful was the naked truth that shone through. Gordon Gekko was a projection of Buddy's own dark desires.

"Buddy? . . . What's going on?" Darien inquired in a faltering voice.

"I been played like a grand piano—by the master, Gekko the Great . . . and today was the big crash. Liquidation sale. He's gonna carve Bluestar into little pieces and sell it all off . . ."

Her tone was melancholy as she carefully picked up the pieces of a precious vase. "I'm sorry. I was afraid something like this could happen."

Fox's face was paler than a white-on-white painting at the Modern. He spoke in a short, winded voice. "Talk about being bent over the sink of life and dry-humped. I handed it to him on a silver platter. I told my father and those people . . ."

"Buddy, it's not your fault, and it's not your decision."

Darien's exculpatory language seemed like a substitute for deep feeling.

"I'm *not* gonna let it happen, Darien."

Bud's voice had suddenly become even and determined, as if despair had galvanized him into a drive for rescue. The color in Darien's cheeks drained. She was paralyzed with fear at the thought of combat with Gordon. Darien had geared her life to be adored by everyone, not to confront someone as powerful as Gekko. While she shared some of Buddy's disappointment, Darien did not intend to join any effort against Gekko to reverse it.

"Don't cross Gordon. He'll crush you. You've worked hard to get where you are. If Gordon doesn't buy Bluestar, someone else will . . . and who's to say they won't do the same thing?"

"At least I wouldn't be pulling the trigger."

Darien's psyche became more threatened with extinction; her nostrils dilated in panic. She ran over to Buddy and tried to shake some sense into him, while also speaking to herself.

"Are you mad! Why are you doing this! We're so close, the town is going to be ours. Don't throw away our future, Buddy!"

Spiritual necessity had unlimited bounds, and he

needed to take some action to snatch the prize from the devil.

"I can stay with the brokerage firm. We can survive without Gordon Gekko."

"I'm not looking to just *survive*. I've been doing that all my life."

"What the hell's that supposed to mean?" There was a painful lack of response.

Darien felt enveloped in danger. She had sought comfort and society with Buddy, not a prescription for self-denial. Fox and Taylor had formed a partnership to satisfy certain needs and ambitions; no passionate love drove nature to overtake reason. Buddy thought, in his imaginary world, that he had shared his most intimate secrets with Darien and she with him; in fact, the relationship's inner life had not advanced since they met.

Darien pulled back from Bud. Her hands were clammy, her body rigid in icy hardness. A dimension of loyalty to Gekko, as well as fear of him, motivated her decision.

"If you make an enemy of Gordon Gekko, I won't be there to stand by you."

Bud expressed his hurt and isolation. "You really mean that? What did he promise you? To take you public? I guess without Gordon's money and seal of approval, I'm not such a hot investment anymore. You're just the best money can buy, Darien."

Darien became coolly remote. *Nature had married what naturally fit,* she thought.

"You're not exactly pure, Buddy. You went after Gekko with the same vengeance you went after me. Look in the mirror before—"

"I'm looking . . . and I sure don't like what I see," he said, staring straight at her.

The truth was, he agreed with her. Youthful suffering had ignited a spark of intellectual clarity. Gordon and Darien were Buddy's tools and instruments, as he was theirs.

Darien collected some things in silence and walked to the door. She paused to consider one final comment.

"Fair enough . . . but I don't want to leave you thinking it's all so simple, Buddy. When I was down and had nothing, it was Gordon who helped me. He got me all my clients, you among them"—she snapped her fingers—"and he can take them away like that. You may find out one day that when you've had money and lost it, it's worse than never having had it at all."

Bud had lost his mentor and lover by his own hand. He had taken almost every wrong turn possible in handling both these relationships, because the goals were wrong. His rage at Darien was equally a painful cry of self-hatred.

"Bullshit! Step out that door, I'm changing the locks."

When there was nothing more to be said, Darien surrendered and walked out.

"You may not believe this, Bud, but I really do

care for you. I think we could've made a good team
. . . but that's how it goes. I'm sorry."

"Get the hell out."

Darien waited by the elevator, staring in the hall
mirror, while Bud reflected in the mirror above the
bar . . . and neither of these young people liked the
person seen there.

$ $ $

When Bud arrived at the office the next morning,
he received the telephone message that all sons
dread.

"Your father had a heart attack. Please come to the
Emergency Room at Elmhurst Hospital."

Bud flagged a cab on Broad Street. "Elmhurst Mu-
nicipal Hospital," he poured out with a sense of urgency.

"Sorry, pal, I don't work Queens."

The next few cabbies gave variations of the theme,
"sorry, off duty," to avoid taking the long trip to
Elmhurst and returning to Manhattan without a fare.
Bud made a quick deal to double the meter and arrived at the emergency room after a seemingly endless ride. He ran through the ER, packed with milling
sufferers and their attendants; it was Babel, where
pain and grieving cried out in equal doses of Hindi,
Spanish, English, Yiddish, and Chinese.

Bud found his mother weeping quietly at the foot
of Carl's bed. It was horrible for Bud to see his dad
in that foreshortened position, feet pointing outward,

leading to a drained and expressionless visage.

"Mom! How is he?"

"He was complaining about chest pains at work. Next thing, he collapsed . . . Oh, Buddy, talk to him, he's so stubborn."

Dominick Amato comforted her, while turning to Bud.

"Doc said he's stable. You can talk to 'im for a few minutes . . . but he's on painkillers."

Bud sat at the head of the bed, enmeshed in a web of IVs, nose catheters, and monitors. He feigned a smile, not hiding his anguish very well.

"Hi ya, Dad . . . I told you never to lift a 747 by yourself."

Carl smiled faintly as Bud spoke. "You gotta pull through, Dad . . . for Mom, for me . . . I guess I never told you—I love you, Dad, I love you more than ever . . ."

Bud sobbed quietly but uncontrollably.

"I didn't mean those things I said to you . . . you're a hero all the way, Dad, you're a rock . . . the best."

Carl's eyes filled with tears as the words gushed out of Buddy's heart.

"And you were right about Gekko, he's one sonofabitch . . . through and through."

Carl began to understand. He was not gleeful at his son's disappointment. Bud continued. "He's gonna break up Bluestar."

Carl's eyes hardened with the chained frustration of Samson.

Buddy was overwhelmed with guilt at what he now had to tell his father, that he'd been right all along.

"Dad, I'm only telling you this now because the pressures of time demand immediate action."

Carl looked at Buddy, anxious, pleading with his eyes.

"I got a plan, Dad, it can work. I can save the airline. I know you got no reason to believe me, but I want you to trust me . . . I need to talk to the unions. Can I speak for you? . . . Your words, not mine!"

Carl reached out weakly to touch Buddy's cheek. He whispered, with total confidence, "I'm proud of you, Buddy. You speak for me, son."

CHAPTER XXI

Bud slid into his father's booth at McGregor's Bar.

Suffering and some residual Queens magic from his upbringing combined to give Buddy the beginning wisdom of maturity. He accepted that it was futile to try to question or modify the perspective of Gordon Gekko; he must expect no hope or mercy from that quarter. *Action* was the only alternative for Buddy's and Bluestar's salvation.

The booth was soon filled by Toni Carpenter, Duncan Wilmore, and Al Tatum. Bud summarized his knowledge about the proposed liquidation of Bluestar, with great humility. Lifetimes spent in adversarial and uncertain environments caused the union leaders to experience less shock than Bud had anticipated. They were determined to find some practical means of thwarting Gekko and listened intently to Buddy's plan.

"The stock's at nineteen and a quarter, and it's going up. Gekko figures by breaking up Bluestar, it's worth at least thirty a share. That means he'll buy up to twenty-three or twenty-four and still anticipate making money."

Duncan Wilmore was puzzled.

"How do you know that the stock will go up?"

"You really don't want to know any more than that, Mr. Wilmore. Let's just say I have some friends."

Wilmore got the drift. "Okay, what happens then?"

Bud spoke with surprisingly little malice toward Gordon. Straight business.

"When the stock hits twenty-three, you guys go to Gekko and lower the boom. Once he learns he has no union concessions, he'll understand that he must suffer large operating losses while trying to implement the plan of liquidation. He'll head for the hills and sell everything he's got."

"Yeah, but who's going to buy the stock then, and what's to prevent another shark from coming along and devouring us?" inquired Toni Carpenter.

"We have an appointment in one hour, which should answer your questions... I think," replied Buddy. "I have a car outside to take us there."

$ $ $

The group emerged from the car on Fifth Avenue. Bud spoke to the doorman. "We have an appointment with Mr. Wildman."

Sir Laurence had a magnificent view of New York from the living-room windows of his impeccably decorated apartment, which had as its canvas the trees, lake, zoo, and rim of fine examples of architecture lining Central Park South and West. An aide to Sir Laurence offered food and beverages, but nobody wanted anything to eat or drink. They sought to get down to business quickly with the imposing figure seated opposite them in a chintz-covered armchair.

Buddy began, "Sir Laurence, what would you say to owning Bluestar Airlines with union concessions —at eighteen a share—and in the process hanging Gordon Gekko out in the wind to twist?"

Wildman leaned back in his chair calmly. "I might be very interested, but why? Why you, mate—I thought you and Gekko were partners?"

Bud showed no emotion.

"Let's just say Mr. Gekko and I have a conflict of interest. I want to see this airline work"—he pointed to the spreadsheets placed before Wildman on the table—"and the figures here show it can work."

Wildman directed his attention to the others, fixing his gaze on each union leader individually. "And you're prepared to take these large salary cuts?"

"We are," said Duncan Wilmore, with the others

nodding their assent, "but we want a contract—iron-clad—that if you buy Bluestar, you can't break it up."

Sir Laurence rocked his head back slightly, with his hands clasped behind it. "I'm still listening. . . ."

$ $ $

Buddy went to Jackson & Steinhem straight from the meeting. His first stop was Marvin Wycoff.

"Bluestar, put all your clients in it . . . and quietly pass the word around the office."

"Thanks, Buddy buddy." His hand hit the switchboard and plugged him into his best institutional client. "Have I got some fancy info for you . . . first call . . ."

Fox entered his office. After brief comments to his secretary, he was glued to the phone with his network of brokers around the world. They were instructed to buy Bluestar at market. Finally, he dialed a familiar number and said in a hushed voice, "Blue Horseshoe loves Bluestar Airlines . . ." The newspaper reporter tried unsuccessfully to engage his anonymous caller in conversation to learn more about BLS being put into play, but he was on his own to verify the story, just as he had been with Anacott Steel and others.

A frenzied crowd of floor brokers surrounded the specialist's window, where a market was made on the New York Stock Exchange in Bluestar shares. The NYSE floor reporter processed transactions as fast as he could punch them into the small computer on the side of the booth; the tape upticked— 20¼; 20½; 21; 21¼. Squads raced across the floor of the Exchange, with new Bluestar buy and sell orders, flashing in and out of the crowd like lightning bugs on a warm summer night. Carl Lewis, veteran specialist, pulled the floor brokers around his booth to get a picture of the stock. He summed up the results with a shout, "I got 400,000 BLS to buy..." in an attempt to bring buyers and sellers together. Sell orders stepped out of the crowd only on significant upticks.

Janet buzzed Bud on the intercom. "Mr. Gekko is on the phone ... himself."

Fox answered Gordon's inquiry with feigned puzzlement. "Yeah. I see it at twenty-two and an eighth, but I don't know what to make of it."

Gekko was concerned about a competitive bid. "The word's out. Your union buddies are talking. Get me in ... and I mean all the way in! Slash and burn, buy everything you can get your hands on. Then call me. When I get the sonofabitch who leaked this, I'm gonna *kill him!*"

He slammed down the receiver, as his eye caught BLS uptick another eighth.

Fox walked onto the Jackson & Steinhem trading floor. Marv was on a high. "The stock's going to Pluto!"

"Start unloading," Buddy said succinctly.

"Sell?" Marv was astonished.

Fox was precise. "Now! Tell everyone to dump!"

When the word spread, brokers frantically called their clients to sell.

$ $ $

At the same time, Gekko paced with a phone in his hand, his lips locked in a grimace, as he searched for answers.

"Who the hell's out there? What are the arbs saying? It's gotta be a big hitter."

Alex responded, apprehensively. "They don't know what's going on! Everybody and his mother is buying; they're out there in force bidding against us."

Natalie entered the office, flustered. "Mr. Gekko, there's a batch of people from Bluestar Airlines outside, demanding to see you."

"What the hell do they want?"

Duncan Wilmore barged in, the point man of an attack force that followed close behind him. "I'd be happy to tell you."

Gekko was surprised but remained calm while Wilmore continued.

"We know what you're up to, Gekko, and let me tell you this"--he bent his close-fisted right arm toward the ceiling and crossed his left forearm in the cleavage—"fuck you! You'll break up Bluestar over my dead body."

Gekko pretended grief at being misunderstood. "You guys must know something nobody else knows. If those are my plans, it's the first I've heard of it."

Toni smiled cynically. "Would you care to put that

in writing . . . on the back of your check?"

Gekko played out his bluff. "I'd like to remind you we already have an agreement, which I expect you to honor."

"Well, in that case I hope you have your pilot's license," jibed Wilmore.

"The reservation system can get awfully screwed up, if we're not paying attention," added Toni in an aw-shucks manner.

Big Al joined the chorus, "And a lot of baggage headed to St. Petersburg could easily find its way to Pittsburgh."

Gekko was furious at being pushed around.

"Listen, you clowns, there's somebody else out there trying to buy your airline; if you want to be Pac-Manned up by Attila the Hun, be my guest!"

Wilmore responded with deep sarcasm. "We'll take our chances. Nice to see you again, Mr. Gekko."

Gekko grabbed his phones, which were lit up like a Christmas tree.

"Yes, Alex?"

"Fox says Bluestar dropped four and a quarter. What do you want him to do?"

Gekko paused, as if to protect his reason against his fury.

"Sell it all . . . what the hell, so I'll only make a few million."

$ $ $

Meanwhile, Wildman had retreated to his yacht in Long Island Sound but remained in constant touch with his broker by radio telephone. He looked at his Quotron as he spoke to the chief equity trader at Ruff.

"Down four and a quarter? I don't know what's going on . . . precisely. I hear Gekko's the buyer. Don't touch it on the way up. If it starts down, buy it only on downticks . . . and very lightly . . . if it hits eighteen, buy whatever's offered."

"Got it!"

Wildman leaned back in his desk chair, amused and relaxed in hopeful anticipation that something good was about to happen to him . . . and something bad to "Gekko the Great."

$ $ $

The specialist on the New York Stock Exchange worked feverishly to make an orderly market in Bluestar, as sellers came out of the woodwork and buyers for small amounts appeared only on downticks. As the stock hit $20, Gordon called a meeting in his office.

"The arbs are getting killed. Where'd the buyers go?" asked Ollie Steeples in a rare moment of total befuddlement.

Alex was very nervous, indeed worried. "We're being devoured, Gordon."

Harold Solomon fearfully addressed Gordon, who

sat somewhat passively with a disconnected telephone receiver dangling over his shoulder. "There's
got to be a way out of this, Gordon."

"Yeah, Harold, why don't you dial 911."

Gekko had no ready answer. He was distraught as
he watched millions pour down an undetectable hole
at the bottom of the pool. He felt like he was giving
an unlimited blood transfusion.

"Fox, where the hell have you been?" he shouted
into the receiver. "I'm losing millions. Look, you got
me into this airline, and you damn well better get me
out. Because if you don't, the only job you're going
to get on the Street is sweeping it! You hear me,
Fox!"

Bud sat in his office at Jackson & Steinhem scrib-
bling an order ticket. He replied without strain, "You
once told me don't get emotional about stock. Gordon, don't. The bid is eighteen and a half and going
down. I hear that there might be a buyer of size at
eighteen. As your broker, I advise you to *take it.*"

Gordon raged uncontrollably, cursing nobody in
particular. Fox held the phone away from his ear and
then shouted with a sense of great urgency.

"Gordon, it's two minutes to the close. I have an
open line to the floor. *What do you want to do?* Decide!"

"Dump it!" mumbled Gordon in the depressed
tone of unconditional surrender.

$ $ $

Wildman's broker stepped out of the crowd at the specialist's window.

"I buy BLS at eighteen."

Gekko's block crossed the tape, as the gong sounded to end New York Stock Exchange trading for the day.

$ $ $

It was a rare occasion when Gekko left the office early enough to watch the six o'clock news. He turned on his thirty-five-inch Sony to catch the business report.

"The big Wall Street story tonight is the roller-coaster ride of Bluestar Airlines. Fueled by takeover rumors, the stock soared as high as twenty-four and an eighth. Then when contradictory rumors later surfaced that the takeover was unfounded, buyers went running for cover, and the stock plummeted to a low of sixteen and a half and closed on a huge block at eighteen."

Gekko watched with a grim countenance, as the announcer went on with the story.

"But then tonight, amid all the scuttlebutt, another rumble shook the Street. According to many sources, raider Sir Laurence Wildman has stepped in and bought a substantial block of Bluestar and is going to announce a deal tomorrow at eighteen that includes the support of the unions."

Gekko absorbed the hard blow. His eyes narrowed

to tiny slits, with only the black dots in his pupils showing, as the pieces of the puzzle fell into place. "Gekko the Great" was the victim of a sucker play! He picked up a heavy ashtray from the cocktail table and hurled it through the Sony screen.

Gekko was crazed. He had known from day one that Fox spelled trouble; nevertheless, he had permitted himself to get into a relationship with an unseasoned youth. Gordon drowned his depression in a double scotch. He couldn't stop wondering whether he had taken an accidental false step or become suicidal in middle age.

$ $ $

There was an unfamiliar silence while Bud crossed the Jackson & Steinhem trading floor to his office. Fox was weary with the wrongs of his recent past; however, he was somewhat rejuvenated by his role in saving Bluestar from sudden death. Chuck Cushing turned quickly away, without a good morning. Marv Wycoff removed his gaze self-consciously to his Quotron, which had a blank screen. Lou Manheim stopped Buddy in the narrow aisle and spoke to him with gruff, fatherly affection.

"Bud, I like you . . . just remember something. Man looks in the abyss, there's nothing staring back at him. At that time, a man finds his character—and that is what keeps him out of the abyss . . ."

"I think I understand what you mean, Mr. Manheim," Bud responded absentmindedly, still trying to absorb the strange tone of his surroundings.

As he entered his office, Janet tried to tell him something, but he cut her off.

"Get my father, will you, Janet."

In Buddy's office, the young SEC investigator who had tracked him down was busy putting government seals on Fox's files. A second man, with a silver badge pinned to a flap that hung from his breast jacket pocket, sat in Buddy's chair using the phone, while a third lawyer-type from the U.S. Attorney's office had a bored look as he peered out of the window. Hy Lynch, standing in remote coldness in the corner of the office, gave Bud a chilling glare when he entered the room.

"He just came in. I'll talk to you later," said Patterson into the telephone.

All three flashed their identifications. Hawkins spoke in a formal manner. "Mr. Fox, you're under arrest for conspiracy to commit securities fraud in interstate commerce and for violating the Insider Trader's Sanction Act."

Patterson read Fox his rights, put his hands behind his back, and clamped handcuffs tightly around Buddy's wrists.

Fox felt the solitude of the damned, as strange hands took possession of him. Buddy suffered such a deep and lonely pain that the sound of his lament could only reach the surface as silence. As Bud was led away, Hy Lynch leaned heavily on his bull's-head cane and hurled a sneering reproach.

"Fox, I knew you were no good right from the beginning."

Fox was led up the narrow trading room aisles. His head bowed lower and lower with dreams of dungeons, as if his vertebrae were collapsing from the weight of his shame. Most of his colleagues removed themselves from direct eye contact with him to avoid sharing in his torment. Buddy had the timeless sorrow of hopelessness etched on his face, as he experienced the isolation of a leper.

The market had opened. Telephones rang crazily off their hooks; stock tickers roamed absentmindedly around the room with nobody to watch them. Death stalked the trading room.

Bud's eyes were red from sobbing when he passed the stunned black receptionist. She managed to utter the slight comfort of the oppressed. "Hang in there, Buddy."

$ $ $

A blanket of rain whipped across the deserted Sheep Meadow in Central Park. The hatless, solitary figure of Gordon Gekko, in a trench coat, stood rigidly on a grassy knoll at its center. Gekko's isolated figure, stark against the gray sky and torrential rain, defined the word "alone." The broad field and splashing mud brought back memories of Campsville.

Gekko was expressionless when he saw Bud Fox walk hesitatingly toward him across the meadow. They faced each other forlornly.

"Hello, Buddy."

"Gordon . . ."

Gekko smiled inscrutably. "You sandbagged me on Bluestar." He raised his eyebrows and furrowed his forehead. "I guess you think you taught the teacher a lesson, that you can make the tail wag the dog, huh?"

Gordon's smile faded.

"When you're through with me, *you're through with everything I'm a part of*. Well, let me cue you in: The ice is melting under your feet, sport . . ."

Without warning, Gordon's eyes flashed the humiliation and hatred of a betrayed lover. Inner rage exploded with his fist smashing into Fox's nose. He twisted Buddy's lapels in his left hand, while slapping Fox's face repeatedly with his right, finally throwing him to the ground. He spoke with the quiet anger of the master to his ungrateful slave as he kicked Fox in the ribs, rolling him through puddles of mud.

"You think you could've gotten this far this fast with anybody else? You think you could be out there dicking somebody like Darien? No, you'd be cold-calling dentists and widows to buy twenty shares of some dog stock! I took you in! A *nobody!* I opened doors for you! I showed you how the system works!"

Fox staggered to his feet, bathed in mud. Blood

gushed over his muddy face, like a swollen spring stream. Gekko ripped open his lip with a left hook; Buddy slumped with the blow, saying nothing, mounting no defense. Gekko raved on, spewing his venom in almost a religious cadence.

"I taught you the value of inside information! How you get it! Anacott Steel. Brant Resources, Geodynamics, Fulham Oil. And this is how you pay me back, you cockroach! I gave you manhood. I gave you everything."

In a vague sense, the victim agreed with his accuser, and Bud almost welcomed his punishment. He got to his knees, swallowing blood, exhausted. Gekko's rage was spent; he breathed hard, almost with pain. As a sign of remorse, he handed Buddy his handkerchief to staunch the flow of blood from his nose and mouth. He whispered softly, regretfully, innocently, "You could've been one of the great ones, Bud . . . I look at you and see myself. . . . Why?"

Bud stared at Gordon, torn by confused emotions of bonds and betrayal.

"I don't know. My dad once told me, money is something you need in case you don't die tomorrow. I guess I realized I'm just Bud Fox. And as much as I wanted to be Gordon Gekko—I'll always be Bud Fox."

He stared longingly at Gordon, trying to say more, tongue-tied with despair. He walked off with tears flowing from his eyes, leaving Gordon standing alone

on the hill with lightning licking the meadow from
the sky.

$ $ $

Astonished patrons of Tavern on the Green, tourists and hard-boiled locals alike, shrunk from the
sight of a young man splattered with blood and mud,
staggering through the elegant front dining area to
reach the bathroom at the back.

Fox stared at his reflection in the mirror while
Harry Hawkins unbuttoned his shirt to retrieve the
microphone taped around his chest. Hawkins and the
FBI agent played back the tapes; Buddy heard Gordon ticking off the deeds and deals they had done
together.

"You did the right thing, Buddy," said Hawkins.

Fox turned away from the abomination in the mirror, feeling sick to his stomach.

$ $ $

The next morning at the opening bell, Lou Manheim, Hy Lynch, and Marv Wycoff stood remarkably
close together, quietly reflecting on the green fluorescent printout of the news ticker.

THE U.S. ATTORNEY'S OFFICE TODAY ANNOUNCED
CRIMINAL CHARGES AGAINST CORPORATE RAIDER
GORDON GEKKO AND STOCKBROKER BUD FOX, FOR
CONSPIRACY TO COMMIT SECURITIES FRAUD, TAX EVA-

SION, VIOLATIONS OF SECURITIES ACTS, AND MAIL FRAUD. MICKEY MORGENSTEIN OF THE SEC ANNOUNCED THAT HE WOULD PERSONALLY TRY THIS IMPORTANT CASE.

CHAPTER XXII

Bud had the vacant eyes and lifeless gait of the condemned when he joined his parents at the small breakfast table in their home. The scars of his difficult passage had not mended.

He appeared somber in a dark blue Macy's suit, red paisley tie, and polished, black Florsheim shoes. Mrs. Fox examined her son in gentle detail, as she would a flower in her garden.

"Don't wear *that* tie, Buddy, it . . ."

His injured expression of encroachment warned that this was not a time for personal commentary.

"A cup of coffee, Buddy?" Carl interjected.

"No, thanks, I'm nervous enough."

Carl leaned back in his chair to check the Timex

clock over the refrigerator on the kitchen wall. "I guess it's time to hit the road."

Bud's muscles tightened. He rose in sad resignation.

"Yeah, I don't want to be late for my own funeral."

The car painfully picked its way across the Fifty-ninth Street Bridge, through sardine-packed rush-hour traffic, headed toward the Foley Square Courthouse at the tip of Manhattan near Wall Street.

Bud was shivering on this warm spring day. Carl spoke supportively, without condescension.

"You told the truth, you gave the money back. All things considered—in this cockamamie world—you're shooting par."

Mrs. Fox offered the reassurance of a mother to her child on the first day of school.

"You helped save the airline, and the people there are gonna remember you for it."

Somehow Buddy's parents felt they had to keep talking to stave off the finality of death.

"If I was you, I'd think about that Bluestar job Wildman's offered you," said Carl.

Bud cut to the marrow. "Dad, I'm going to jail and you know it."

Carl shook his head dejectedly but soberly, absorbing the terrible hurt of the words alone.

"Maybe that's the price, Bud, maybe so. It's gonna be rough on you, but maybe in some screwed-up way, that's the best thing that can happen to you.

Stop chasing the big bucks and go *produce* something with your life, *create*, don't live off the buying and selling of others . . ."

Bud's mother added, with the genuine confidence of experience with her son, "You can do it, Bud. Once you set your mind to something, I believe *you* can do anything in the world. . . . We *got* to do it for ourselves."

Bud stared straight ahead, motionless.

They arrived at Foley Square.

"We'll park the car and catch up with you," said Carl.

Bud was the definition of defeat, climbing the steep, indifferent granite steps of the United States Courthouse.

"It's too late, but I get it now . . . what Lou Manheim was saying," he reflected dejectedly. "I was part of something on Wall Street . . . part of another something back where I came from . . . and I sold myself out for a hollow obsession."

Buddy's youth was a light shining faintly through his blackest night at the bottom of the abyss. A small voice deep inside him countered his despair. . . . "Now I can begin."

Outstanding fiction in paperback from Grafton Books

Nicholas Salaman

The Frights	£2.50	☐
Dangerous Pursuits	£2.50	☐

Salman Rushdie

Grimus	£2.50	☐

Denise Gess

Good Deeds	£2.50	☐

Lisa Zeidner

Alexandra Freed	£2.50	☐

Ronald Frame

Winter Journey	£2.50	☐

Torey Hayden

The Sunflower Forest	£2.95	☐

Cathleen Schine

Alice in Bed	£2.50	☐

Doris Grumbach

The Ladies	£2.50	☐

C J Koch

The Year of Living Dangerously	£2.95	☐
The Doubleman	£2.95	☐

John Treherne

The Trap	£2.50	☐

To order direct from the publisher just tick the titles you want
and fill in the order form.

Outstanding American fiction in paperback from Grafton Books

John Fante

Wait until Spring, Bandini	£2.50	☐
Ask the Dust	£2.50	☐
Dreams from Bunker Hill	£2.50	☐

Ron Hansen

The Assassination of Jesse James by the Coward Robert Ford	£2.95	☐

Walker Percy

The Movie Goer	£2.50	☐
The Last Gentleman	£2.95	☐
The Second Coming	£2.95	☐

To order direct from the publisher just tick the titles you want and fill in the order form.

The best in biography from Grafton Books

Larry Collins and Dominique Lapierre
Or I'll Dress You in Mourning   £1.25 ☐

Ladislas Farago
Patton: Ordeal and Triumph   £2.95 ☐

Hermann Hesse
Autobiographical Writings   £2.95 ☐
A Pictorial Biography (illustrated)   £1.50 ☐

A E Hotchner
Papa Hemingway   £1.25 ☐

Doris Lessing
In Pursuit of the English   £1.95 ☐

Stan Gébler Davies
James Joyce – A Portrait of the Artist (illustrated)   £2.50 ☐

Jean Stein and George Plimpton
Edie: An American Biography (illustrated)   £3.95 ☐

Leonard Mosley
Zanuck (illustrated)   £4.95 ☐

To order direct from the publisher just tick the titles you want
and fill in the order form.

All these books are available at your local bookshop or newsag or can be ordered direct from the publisher.

To order direct from the publishers just tick the titles you want fill in the form below.

Name _____

Address _____

Send to:
Grafton Cash Sales
PO Box 11, Falmouth, Cornwall TR10 9EN.

Please enclose remittance to the value of the cover price plus:

UK 60p for the first book, 25p for the second book plus 15p per c for each additional book ordered to a maximum charge of £1.90.

BFPO 60p for the first book, 25p for the second book plus 15p copy for the next 7 books, thereafter 9p per book.

Overseas including Eire £1.25 for the first book, 75p for second b and 28p for each additional book.

Grafton Books reserve the right to show new retail prices on cove which may differ from those previously advertised in the text elsewhere.